NOW I LAY ME
DOWN TO SLEEP

Where Was God When the Lights Went Out?

—— Mona Green ——

www.monagreen.com
(E-Mail) monagreen52@yahoo.com

Copyright © 2010 Mona Green
All rights reserved.

ISBN-10: 1449928757
EAN-13: 9781449928759

This book is dedicated to my mother, Vernella Chambers (1932–1984). Her loving kindness taught me how to be original.

This book is dedicated to my loving father, Rev. John Chambers, who taught me how much smoother life can be when I smile. Many thanks go to my wonderful husband, Willie R. Green Jr., who has been very supportive and understanding through the journeys of my writing. I could not have completed this work without him.

I thank my children, Jereme, Kyle, and Ray, for believing in me and giving me consideration for writing when I needed it. I want to extend special thanks to my dearest cousin Pamela Barnes Paul for her input and encouragement and countless hours helping to make this book a success. Pamela, I just want to thank you for reading my book with me. You are truly one of God's gifts to me.

Lot of appreciation goes out to my wonderful relatives, friends, and coworkers for encouraging me to pursue my dreams.

I would like to thank Elder J. T. Miller for introducing me to Sharel Love.

Many thanks to Sharel Love for helping me restructure my work. Your advice was very helpful.

Special thanks go to Dr. Peggy Brook-Bertram, co-founder of the Uncrowned Queens Institute for Research and Education on Women Inc. at the University of Buffalo. Thank you, Dr. Bertram, for reading my book and sharing your comments. I am truly grateful for you sharing my story on your Web page. Your interest in me and how we met will always be a special miracle to let me know that this book was meant to be written.

I would like to express gratitude to Sandra Terrell for helping my puzzle of grammar be what it should. Although you are retired, you still make a wonderful teacher.

I would like to acknowledge and thank Publishing Consultant, Zach J. Coddington for accepting my manuscript. I would like to give many thanks to the Createspace editors, interior book design, and cover design for all of their suggestions, hard work, and professionalism. I also give a special thanks to The Createspace Project Team 1 for being able to answer all my questions and being a true problem solver.

Upcoming:

Curse of the Mosley Women: *The Lyre*

TABLE OF CONTENTS

INTRODUCTION

There was a time in my life I thought fear would be the death of me. For most of my childhood I was tormented by tales of unseen creatures of the night. Of course there were no such creatures, but what did I know? The anticipation of meeting them was always a dark room away.

I was taught to pray, "If I die before I wake, I pray the Lord my soul to take." For the Lord to take my soul was one thing; for the creatures of the night to get me was another. Either way, I always saw little hope for tomorrow and I was afraid to go to sleep. Each night, fear stole my peace and kidnapped my sweet dreams.

As obvious as it may sound, it takes a lifetime of lessons to remember that there is nothing to fear but fear itself.

Most of my fears were silly, but at the time, being afraid was the only choice I knew. Fear was once my bondage; how I overcame it is my testimony.

The reason I wrote this story is to bring awareness to how unsettled childhood fears can manifest into greater fears. My fears were almost like an addiction. I was always afraid of something. For many years, fear paralyzed me like a stun gun during my hours of sleep. Some of my fears were as good as taking a lazy pill because they held me back from becoming my best. I thank God that I can now find a little humor in what I feared, and I hope that many of my stories will evoke similar humorous memories to each reader.

CHAPTER 1

THE BASEMENT

In 1956, when I was four years old, our family lived in a town called Stony Brook. My whole world centered around my father, mother, brother, and me; and, of course, the place where we lived on Pine Street. Our house's natural elements consisted of all kinds of trees with the exception of pine; as for me, the willow trees were the easiest to identify. Other than a shortcut to get across town, Pine Street did not have much to offer. Occasionally tires of a car could be heard as it rolled over the graveled road. With the exception of the moon and the stars at night, our house gave the street its only source of light.

Our cube-shaped house was covered with mismatched shingles, giving it an appearance of poor patchwork. The overhang on the front porch looked like it was about to collapse, the spring on the front door was squeaky, and needless to say, the floorboards were in much need of repair. The house was divided into two living quarters, 6A and 6B. Spanish-speaking tenants lived in the main part of the house. Alongside the house was a foyer that led to the basement, and that is where we lived.

The kitchen had a huge black iron stove. It was used to cook our meals and heat the house. For fuel Daddy used charcoal and wood. He got most of our wood from the trees on Pine Street.

Our basement apartment stayed flooded with water. To keep our feet from getting wet, Daddy built wooden skids and placed them throughout the basement floor. The two windows in the basement gave us some daylight during the day; otherwise our only source of light came from our television set and two bare light bulbs. One light bulb hung in the kitchen area and the other where we slept. Usually one bulb burned at a time.

The back yard of our basement apartment had a very uninviting outhouse. During the day, sunlight would shine through the missing planks, and at night we would use a flashlight or a candle.

Mommy was always busy doing household chores, and caring for everyone was a full-time job. Her name was Vera, but Daddy called her "V." Being that our basement was always filled with water, Mommy often said the dampness in the basement was what gave us runny noses. The basement was also filled with shadows. Mommy entertained my brother and me by making more shadows from the motion of her hand. The rabbit and bird shadows made me uncomfortable.

My only sibling was my two-year-old brother, Joel Jr. We called him Winky on account that his right eye did not open too well. His episodes of coughing spells often led to frightful nose bleeds, so Mommy did her best to keep him calm and quiet.

My first name is Mona, and Lisa is not my middle name, although most people insist that it is. It used to bother me, but now I don't mind. My real name is Mona Fay Cartman, and I don't mind smiling about that.

For a short while we owned a cocker spaniel. She had short, wavy black hair. When she was given to us she had a lot of ticks so Daddy named her Ticky. Daddy used his Boy Scout skills to get rid of her ticks with his pocket knife. I don't believe there were any ticks that stood up to the heated blade of Daddy's pocket knife. I was forewarned not to pet Ticky, and yet I petted her anyway. The last time I petted her was on a hot summer day. It must have been real hot because she struck me with her paw. Her nail drew blood from right below my lower left eyebrow, and to this day I bear the scar. I never believed that it was Ticky's intent to hurt me, but Mommy insisted that Daddy take her for a one-way ride. I begged them to keep her and promised not to pet her, but Daddy put Ticky in the car anyway and took her for a ride. Although I never saw Ticky again, I continued to hope for her return.

Most of my amusement came from playing with my dolls and watching television cartoons and children's programs. I also found TV commercials to be very entertaining. My other great amusement came from listening to the quarrels of the Spanish-speaking tenants that lived in the upper part of the house. Although we didn't speak Spanish, I still found them to be amusing.

Whenever I heard them talking or arguing, that was where I made my ring-side seat. I don't think Mommy found them entertaining at all. Often when they got loud, she would clench her teeth to say, "I'll be so glad when those people move."

Each time I heard those words, I would ask, "Why do you want them to leave, Mommy?"

Her answer was always the same: "When they move out, that is where we are going to live."

Daddy said our landlord, Mrs. Hawkins, lived high on the hog. He said she also owned a chicken farm. However, what we lived in looked more like a place for her chickens. Our house was one of many others she owned and rented for her own capital gain.

Daddy always paid his rent on time. Often Mrs. Hawkins came twice a month to collect for her lucky jackpot, but Daddy was the lucky one because he always kept his rent receipts. In conversation Mrs. Hawkins always called Daddy Joel. That was his first name.

As a child Daddy seemed much taller than he is now. He referred to himself as being average height. Although Mommy stood about five feet six inches, he stood about an inch and a half shorter than her. Daddy was muscular, his shoulders were broad, and his upper torso was shaped like a V. He always had a little bounce in his walk that could be noticed a mile away. His eyebrows arched like a mountain, which made his thoughts more readable. Except for his mustache, he did not keep much hair on his face. His nostrils were much wider than Mommy's nose. His skin was more like the color of walnut and Mommy's complexion was about a half shade darker.

Making fifty cents an hour was not exactly living large, but it kept food on the table and a roof over our heads and clothes on our backs. Daddy worked for a chemical company named Galco. On weekends he also worked at a restaurant where he parked cars for the customers.

The tips he received enabled him to save money. For one hundred dollars he purchased land in a town called Mulberry. His dream was to build a house that we could live in and call our very own.

MOVING UP

It took about one year for the people upstairs to move out of the house. On the day they moved out, we moved upstairs to 6A Pine Street, just as Mommy hoped we would.

The living room of our new living quarters was just past the front door. Off to the left was my shared bedroom, and straight ahead was the kitchen. To the left of the kitchen was the bathroom, and to the right of the kitchen was the area where Mommy washed our clothes. Straight through the kitchen was the entrance to my parents' bedroom.

During the day the sunlight flowed from room to room. It felt good to live in a house that had dividing walls. I also felt privileged to live in a house that had a real bathroom with a real toilet that made life simpler and more pleasurable when taking care of personal needs.

There was no means of hot running water; therefore, we had to boil our water in order to get a decent Saturday night bath.

The house itself had two sources of heat. In one corner of our living room stood a pot-belly iron stove, and the kitchen also had an iron stove, but it was wider and was used to cook our meals. Alongside the cooking stove was always an ample supply of coal and wood that Daddy used for fuel. Every week he purchased several pounds of coal. Daddy was very strong because he carried it all in a burlap bag. If there was enough money, he would also buy wood, but if he didn't, then he'd find a tree and chop it himself.

The front porch was always my favorite part of the house. When we lived in the basement, I was not allowed to go near that front porch. When it became available to us, I was allowed to play on it, but I wasn't allowed to leave it. Standing on the steps of the front porch always gave me a panoramic view of our front lawn.

While we were moving out from the basement, a family in a truck sat waiting patiently to move in. The family who would move into the basement apartment was a man, a woman, and a young girl. The man's name was Sam, his wife's name was Miss Judy, and their daughter's name was Sandra.

Sam was a good size taller than Daddy, and his face looked rough, as if it had not been shaven in a few days. His complexion was a bit lighter than Daddy's. I don't believe Sam could have ever sneaked up on anyone because his breath always reeked with the smell of whiskey.

Miss Judy had hair down to her back. She had the same complexion as Sam. She would have looked prettier if she smiled sometimes. Her expression always seemed flat. Miss Judy loved cigarettes; she would sometimes have one lit before finishing the other.

Their daughter Sandra stood a little taller than me and looked almost twice my age. Although her frame was kind of frail, she had the most beautiful set of green eyes. Sandra did not look anything like her rough-faced daddy. She was very pretty with long, wavy hair.

Sam and his wife were always yelling. Sandra was always crying. When Sam got angry he would hit and kick at whatever was in his way. Winky and I did not know any better; we got a kick out of putting our ears to the floor to hear whatever we could hear.

Christmas came shortly after we moved in. Winky and I had a good Christmas that year. Santa brought him a holster set with toy guns and me a doll that could make tears. I was so happy when I received that doll that I hardly took notice of the other gifts under our Christmas tree.

Winky and I played happily with our toys until we heard a cry that came from outside of the house. Mommy said it sounded like Sandra. I thought she might have fallen in the snow or on the ice. I ran to my bedroom window to see what I could see, but what I heard was what shocked me.

"I told you before and I am telling you again, you ain't getting nothing for Christmas! So shut up!"

How could that have happened? How did Santa forget her? Santa was generous to me and my brother. Why did Sam have to sound so mean? That was the first time I remember my heart breaking for someone.

A few days after that Christmas, Winky was diagnosed with acute bronchitis. He was hospitalized for a short while, and of course my heart went out to him. When he came home, Mommy had her hands full. She catered to his whims because she did not want him to become exhausted, but in most cases she looked like the one who was exhausted.

CHAPTER 2

THE SUPERNATURALS

One cold winter morning while Mommy was sleeping late, I took advantage of not being supervised. Indulging in exercises that Mommy prohibited was fun. Jumping up and down on the living room sofa also helped to keep some of those goose bumps off of my arms and some of the chatter off of my teeth. Winky joined me; we had a great time until he accidentally tipped the lamp and caused it to fall. He came very close to falling himself. It must have startled him because he began to cough. I patted his back the way I had seen Mommy do many times. While patting his back, I touched his foot with my free arm and found it to be very cold, and his diaper looked a little heavy, emitting the smell of ammonia.

When his coughing subsided, I coaxed him into quietly playing with one of my dolls. At that point I knew something was wrong because the house had really cooled down. I was cold and my brother felt cold and wet, and I knew he must have been hungry.

Mommy was in her last stages of pregnancy. I knew she wasn't feeling well, but I didn't know how ill she was. I felt it was time to find out why she was still in bed. As I walked from the living and through the kitchen, I looked around to see if there was anything to eat. A cracker can was on the table, but as much as I wanted to nibble, I felt it was more important to check on Mommy.

Her bedroom door was slightly open when I peeked in on her. As soon as my hand touched the knob of her bedroom door I sensed something was wrong. I could see that she was still in the bed and her back was facing the door. I called out to her, but she did not answer. I thought she was asleep so I walked around to the side of the bed where I could see her face. I started to shake her, but from what I could see, she was already shaking. Perspiration was all about her face and on her pillow.

Her eyes were slightly open. I stood before her to make eye contact, but for some reason it felt like another set of eyes was watching me. Keeping my eyes only fixed on her, I asked, "Mommy, do you want water?"

Her only response was the groans that came from her throat. At that point I felt helpless and scared for her life.

I looked about the room as if someone else was in there. What I saw didn't make sense: light was coming from one side of the room, and some form of darkness came from the other side. Although Mommy didn't really see me, I knew something else did. I felt as though a battle was taking place in that room; it felt like death, and I knew she was fighting for her life.

To help her win the battle, I felt the need to pray. The prayer "Now I lay me down to sleep" came to my mind. At the time it was the only prayer I knew. I did not want to pray that prayer because I did not want to say "If I die before I wake." As a matter of fact, I didn't want to think about death; I only wanted to think about life. I couldn't stay in that room any longer. I could hardly breathe from the overwhelming sensation of fear and sadness. Without realizing it, I had backed my way out to the living room.

After sitting on the sofa I began to rock back and forth, wondering what I should do next.

Winky appeared to be content while he played with one of my dolls, so there was no sense in getting him alarmed; he was almost three years old and I was almost five. He was too young to understand. I too was barely old enough to understand exactly what was going on. The one thing I knew for sure was that Mommy was very sick and needed help.

On the wall above the couch hung the Ten Commandments. They were written in golden glitter on a dark blue cardboard plaque. Often when scolding me, Mommy would point to the sparkling letters and remind me that God was watching me.

As I looked upon the plaque I wondered: if God could see me when I was bad, then maybe He could see when I was good. Although I didn't know how to read that plaque, I felt that its sparkles were reading me. While facing the back rest of the sofa, I held my hands together and knelt to my knees to pray. I kept my eyes fixed upon those sparkles as if all that glittered was God's eyes.

"God, please don't let anything happen to Mommy. Please help her and please bring Daddy home soon. Amen."

I honestly believed that God had heard my prayer. Whatever was watching me in Mommy's room gave me the feeling that God was not that far away.

After praying, not only did I feel better, I was able to think more clearly. I remembered Mommy applying a cool, wet wash cloth to Winky's forehead when he had a fever, so I thought that if I ran cold water on her wash cloth and applied it to her forehead, it would make her feel better. I felt very nervous about going back to that bedroom.

The house began to feel cold due to the fact that the fire in the stove no longer crackled and popped. The water from the faucet was ice cold and made my hands even colder, but Mommy was the one who was sick, and that, of course, was more important. After squeezing out the wash cloth, I proceeded to walk by only looking down where my feet led me. While I was walking through the kitchen the telephone rang, but since it was in the living room, I did not answer it. Besides, it had only been a short while ago that the operator informed Mommy that I was playing on the phone. For that I got a good spanking, so I allowed the phone to ring and ring. I thought if God was watching then perhaps the telephone operator was watching too.

Until I reached Mommy's bedside, I kept my eyes on my feet. To watch her suffer made my heart ache, but the fact that she was still alive gave me the greatest relief. While applying the wash cloth to her forehead, I thought I saw a beam of light coming from the corner of my eye. I was sure that it was not the sun because it was like a light I had never seen before. I was afraid more for Mommy's life than for mine. I did not want that light to take her away from me.

While dabbing the wash cloth over her face, she opened her eyes. Although her eyes connected with mine, I knew in my heart that she still did not see me. I was so glad that she was still breathing. As bad as they might sound, her painful groans sounded more hopeful than a questionable silence. As her tears fell to the sides of her temples, my heart prayed for her life.

I didn't want to leave Mommy's side, but I became concerned as I listened to Winky's feet pitter patter around the kitchen floor. To ensure his safety, I left Mommy's side to check on him. He stood in front of the ice box and banged on its door. When I opened the door to the ice box, I was relieved to see that there was still a bottle of milk left from the milk man. Carefully I took the bottle from the ice box for two reasons: the bottle was made of glass and I did not want to waste the milk. After getting the milk into our glasses I opened the cracker can. We helped ourselves till we were satisfied.

After getting our stomachs filled, I led Winky to the living room sofa. The only way to keep him still was to sit with him.

I told myself, "If I keep real still, everything will be alright." Over and over I said to myself, "Be still."

I had no way of measuring time, but I knew I sat there long enough to know that my being still was the key to hearing Daddy's keys jingle as he unlocked the front door of the house. When he came in the door, I wanted him to lift me up and put me on his shoulders the way he normally did when coming through the door, but the look on his face told me that this was not the time. As he walked by, he patted me dearly on top of my head and asked if I was alright. Without waiting for an answer he reached for Winky and lifted him in the air.

The look on Daddy's face went from a concerned look to a worried look. I followed close behind him as he carried my brother to Mommy's bedside. Daddy called out to her, but she didn't answer. After he took a look at her, he directed me to go to my bedroom to get me and my brother's coat and hat. After I returned from our bedroom with our belongings, he changed Winky's diaper and dressed him. Rather than fuss with Winky's coat he wrapped him in a blanket. Daddy carried my brother while leading me to the car. He placed us in the front seat. After he settled us in, he somehow managed to get Mommy to the car and had her lie in the back seat of his 1929 black Dodge.

STILLBORN

After arriving at the hospital, Mommy did not stay in the emergency room. The doctor ordered that she be taken to the upper part of the hospital right away to have her baby. Daddy, Winky, and I were also sent to the upper part of the hospital with her but had to stay in the waiting room.

The waiting room seemed more than just a waiting room. It was a place to learn how to sit still and be quiet. Daddy had already warned me not to say a word. He said that we had to be quiet because we were in the hospital.

After Daddy settled us into the waiting room, he took out a cigarette to smoke. His hands seemed a little shaky. He kept the heel of his foot off the floor while his knee went rapidly up and down. The look from his eyes reminded me to sit still and be quiet. Although Daddy did not say a word, his nervousness could be easily seen. I suppose this was one example of actions speaking louder than words. As he smoked, his eyes moved rhythmically about the room, from the entrance of the room to the clock on the wall, to me, my brother, and back to the entrance.

A huge silver radiator about half as tall as Daddy, with a width as long as his arms, stood across from where we sat. Every so often a burst of steam hissed from its plumbing nozzle. In spite of all that heat, the waiting room had a peculiar, uncanny chill.

High on the wall above the radiator hung a large clock, its mechanism humming rhythmically throughout the room. Although I didn't know how to tell time, that did not stop me from looking at its second hand going around and around. Of course the more the second hand moved, the more it felt like time was standing still.

Right under the clock hung a wooden cross with a figure of a bronze-colored man with briars around his head. The sadness on his face also made me feel sad. Even though the upper part of his body was bare, the weight of the world seemed to be right upon his shoulders.

There was nothing much to look at other than the sofa with a wooden coffee table in front of it that held a magazine, a Bible, and an ashtray. The magazine looked like it may have had some interesting pictures. The Bible appeared to be aged and yet barely touched. The ashtray looked like an object that could be spun in a circle. Being curious, I wanted so badly to see if that Bible had pictures similar to the cross that hung on the wall. I tapped Daddy on his arm and pointed to the Bible and then to the magazine. Gathering from the look on his face I decided to just keep still.

After what seemed to be hours, a doctor and two nurses walked into the waiting room. With much anticipation, Daddy stood on his feet to hear the heralding of these three messengers. Just to look at them dressed in uniforms made me feel nervous. There were no smiles. Their silence echoed that there was something wrong. The doctor momentarily stood in the doorway with one arm across his chest and the other pointing toward his chin.

Finally the doctor pointed to one nurse, indicating that she should be the one to sit with me and my brother, and then he pointed to the other nurse, indicating that she would be the one to assist him. The doctor signaled his finger for Daddy to step outside the room. Daddy turned toward me and pointed at me in a language of his own. His message was clear: I was to remain there until he came back. He put his finger vertically to his lips and then pointed to Winky.

As I remained seated I wondered about the familiarity of the nurse who sat with us. After she looked at my brother, who was still sleeping like an angel, her face looked as if she had seen a ghost. Perhaps she remembered him from one of his previous hospitalizations.

As she sat with us, she hardly moved a muscle. From what I could observe, she reminded me of the picture of the nurse on the shoe-polish box, except this nurse did not seem quite as friendly. I could not help but stare at her white face. She wore a white turtle-looking hat on her head and also had on a white uniform dress. Her white shoes had clean white laces and her white nylon stockings had seams along the backs of her legs.

She wore eyeglasses that sat on her nose. The lenses made her eyes appear very large. I tried not to stare at her, but I couldn't help it. The lenses of her glasses magnified her eyes like the granny glasses on the big bad wolf in the story of "Little Red Riding Hood." I wanted to say to her, "Miss Nurse, what big eyes you have." She offered a plasticity of a smile that matched the peculiar, uncanny chill that remained in the room.

Shortly after making my own personal observation of that nurse, Daddy returned. The look on his face was very much like the look of the man that hung on the cross. Daddy too looked like he had the weight of the world on his shoulders. This was the first time I remembered seeing him look sad and worried.

The nurse who sat with me and my brother slipped away as Daddy gathered my hat and coat. Winky was still sleeping. Silence rang out in that waiting room long enough; I had questions and I couldn't hold my peace any longer.

"Daddy, what's the matter? Where is Mommy?"

"Your mommy is very sick, she needs a lot of rest and she will have to stay in the hospital till she's better."

"Where is Mommy's baby?"

"The baby died, stillborn."

"What is stillborn?"

"The baby was born dead."

"Why? How did the baby die?

"It was God's will. The baby is in heaven."

It was hard for me to understand why Daddy seemed so overwhelmed. Didn't God spare Mommy? To me that was more important than losing her to a stillborn baby I had yet to see.

Mommy came close to losing her life. She never laid eyes on her baby. Daddy said the baby looked just like him. Private funeral arrangements were made. Daddy was the only attendant, besides the funeral owners.

Although I never saw my stillborn brother, it felt as if I had seen him; perhaps I did, maybe it was in a dream. Anyway, I have a mental picture of him that stays forever posted upon the walls of my heart.

I remember hearing Mommy reciting one of the verses to the Twenty-third Psalm. I heard her say, "Although I walk through the valley of the shadow of death, I will fear no evil." Prior to her coming to the hospital, I believe it was death that I felt in my parents' bedroom. I believe death was that strange chill that lingered in that hospital waiting room. I believe that the silence in that waiting room was the whispers of death. I also believe that Mommy walked through the valley of the shadow of death.

Up to that point I had never considered the valley of the shadow of death as an issue, but surely death had now made its statement. Mommy came very close to losing her own life as she labored to bring her stillborn baby into this life. It was through him that I learned how fragile life can be. It brought me no comfort to know that the threat of death was more certain than the promise of life. For some people, going to the hospital may only be a one-way trip. Sadly, for my stillborn brother, his trip came to an end before his life ever began.

While Mommy was hospitalized, my brother and I stayed with Daddy's sister. I don't think Winky cared for the way Aunt Kate potty-trained him. Her switch that she used to spank him worked like a magic wand. By the time Mommy was ready to come back home, Winky did not need his diapers anymore.

Although it was only a few weeks, Mommy's hospitalization seemed to last forever. I believe Aunt Kate was just as happy as we were about Mommy coming home. I felt so grateful to have Mommy home again. She was still weak when she arrived, but to me that didn't matter because we were a family again.

In her absence I thought I had done some growing up so I offered to wash the dishes, but the sink was too high. Daddy built a step stool so that I could wash the dishes over the kitchen sink. Washing dishes was fun! I think I spent more time playing in the dish water than washing the dishes. Winky was just as happy as I was to have Mommy back. In fact, he thought he could go back to being diapered until he felt the magic of Mommy's branchy wand. After Mommy became stronger, Daddy continued building the house that he said we would live in some day.

CHAPTER 3

THE INVISIBLES

Mommy owned a vanilla cream-colored comb made of hard rubber. It was her favorite comb and she used it for two reasons: to comb our hair and to tap my legs when I misbehaved. When she used the comb for my misbehaving, the comb gave an appearance of having lots of power like fan blades moving through the air.

Misbehaving was something I tried not to do too often because Mommy said she had eyes behind her head and she could see everything I did. At first I didn't believe her and I needed to know more.

"Mommy, I don't see eyes behind your head."

"Of course you can't see them, they are invisible."

"Invisible? What is that?"

"Invisible is something you can't see."

Visible or invisible...eyes behind the head were scary and I hoped to never see them. Her invisible eyes got me thinking about what else might be invisible in that house. On the morning before she went to the hospital I had a feeling that something invisible was in her bedroom.

One evening Mommy asked me if I wanted to comb her hair. Normally I would have loved to do so, but now that Mommy had invisible eyes it made me see things differently.

"No, Mommy, I would rather comb Susie's hair." Susie was one of my favorite dolls.

"Come here and comb my hair. I want you to grease my scalp." I nearly froze when she held out her favorite comb for me to use.

"Come here, girl." I just froze where I stood. I was so afraid that I could not move.

"Why are you just standing there?"

"Mommy, do you really have eyes behind your head?"

"Yes, but you can't see them. Now get up on the couch and let me show you how to grease my scalp."

She showed me how to part and grease her scalp. In hopes of running out of grease before getting to the back of her head, I strategically emptied the jar of grease to only the top and side of her scalp.

"Mommy, there is no more grease."

"What do you mean? It was over half a jar! All you needed was a little grease!"

Mommy took the comb and I handed her the jar. She took one look at that empty jar and took a deep breath. I thought she was going to hit me with the comb but instead she had me scoop the extra globs of grease from her scalp and return it back in the jar.

After getting the extra globs of grease back into the jar, I asked, "Mommy, I'm sleepy now, can I go to bed?"

"You can be sleepy all you want, but you are going to grease the back of my scalp."

It was the manner in which she held the comb that gave me all the encouragement I needed to get started. I would have rather been in the position of taking the comb from her than having her keep the comb and apply it to my legs for making her wait. After finishing the last section of her hair, I gave her back the comb.

"Now massage my scalp."

Eek! I did not want to massage her scalp. I barely made it when I greased it. I suppose this would have been the perfect time to poke those invisible eyes right out of her head, but how could I poke at something I couldn't see?

Again she repeated, "Massage my hair!"

The way Mommy held that comb was all the inspiration I needed. It would have been an honor and a joy to do her hair, but the thought of a pair of eyes connected to the back of her head took the fun out of doing the deed.

That night after saying my "Now I lay me down to sleep" prayers, I got in the bed and Mommy turned off the light. While lying there, I tightly closed my eyes and imagined her invisible eyes looking like negative photo film, visible yet transparent. Needless to say I felt uncomfortable and scared. In the bed, I had my brother and my doll. As for my brother, his eyes were shut, but Susie's eyes were halfway open. Even with them closed, I no longer cared for her company while I slept. From that night on Susie slept face down in the toy box located at the end of my bed.

That night I found many reasons to get out of bed. My request for extra snacks was denied. Several trips to the bathroom to drink water led to several trips to release it.

The volume of the television was always loud enough for me to hear. I loved singing along with all the commercial jingles. Some of my favorites were, "Winston tastes smokes good like a cigarette should," and of course, "Charlie says I love my Good and Plenty" and Brylcreem, a little dab will do you." I suppose I got a little carried away in singing along with some of those jingles.

I must have gotten too loud because I heard Mommy's shoes sliding across the living room floor like sandpaper on wood. Quickly I pulled the covers snug around my neck, closed my eyes, and pretended to be asleep. I could hear her mumbling certain words as she got closer to my bedroom door. Her footsteps stopped at the opening of my bedroom door and as she spoke I could feel her staring at me.

"You better go to sleep before the *Sand-Man* catches you awake."

There was no way I was going to let her walk away without telling me who the *Sand-Man* was.

"Mommy...Who is the *Sand-Man?*"

"He puts sand in children's eyes that don't go to sleep when they're told."

"Mommy, can I go to sleep with you?"

"No! Why do you want to sleep with me?"

"I'm scared of the *Sand-Man*, Mommy."

"Just go to sleep or the *Sand-Man* will get you."

At this point I felt afraid and unsafe. How could I go to sleep with the *Sand-Man* on the loose? Why was he allowed free passage in our home? Daddy was not home because he was working at our future home. If Mommy could not protect me from the *Sand-Man* then who could?

"Please, Mommy, can I sleep with you?"

"No, just go to sleep."

"Mommy, could you leave the light on?"

"Okay, but you still better go to sleep."

On the wall across from where I lay hung a plaque of the Twenty-third Psalms. It was similar to the plaque of the Ten Commandments that hung in the living room. Keeping my eyes fixed upon the gold lettering, without making a sound, I moved my lips singing the "Jesus Loves Me" song until I fell asleep.

Daddy was the eighth of nine children. He said his daddy used to build houses for a living. The skills he learned from his father and the skills he mastered from working at Galco enabled him to accomplish the task of building his own home and working on his own automobile. During the day Daddy continued to work at Galco. When getting off work, he often drove straight to Mulberry to work on our new home. He was always working, but when he was home, he always found the time to play with me. Often he'd bring home a novelty toy for Winky and me. He said when he was a child his parents could not afford toys. Giving us toys not only made my brother and me smile, but it made him smile too.

When Daddy was home he was either working on his car or resting. Often while napping, he would utter numbers taken from ruler measurements. To hear him talk while he slept made me laugh, especially when I heard him trying to correct himself. Each night before retiring to bed, I would sit on his lap. Daddy never made mention of the *Sand-Man*. I always felt safe in his strong, gentle, loving arms. He always held me till I fell asleep, and then he would carry me to bed.

CHAPTER 4

EAGER BEAVERS

My favorite television program was *Rumpus Room*. The show was a preview of kindergarten. The *Rumpus Room* teacher's name was Miss Joann. She was famous for teaching preschoolers in an entertaining way. Every child wanted to be on her show. She called her students "Eager Beavers." A make-believe forest was the theme setting for the show. The program activities included singing, story time, and playing musical logs. For a snack the children ate cookies and drank milk. Before eating anything they always said a prayer of thanks. Miss Joann always closed out her program saying,

> Eager Beavers all of you!
> Who is working?
> Please tell me do!
> Did all my beavers
> Work and play?
> Or
> Did all of my beavers run away?"

Immediately after that, she held a telescope to one of her eyes and pointed it at the television camera and named each child that she claimed to see.

Each day I listened carefully for my name. Many times I heard her say "Lisa" but never "Mona." Not ever hearing my name was always disappointing and left me feeling as if I didn't exist. I thought perhaps her telescope needed to be adjusted. After all, Mommy never had a problem locating me because she had her own personal set of invisible eyes.

It was the school year of 1957 when Mommy registered me for kindergarten. I was excited about this new adventure in my life. I felt just as prestigious as any Eager Beavers aired on *Rumpus Room*.

My school clothes were picked from the Sears catalog. Mommy ordered five dresses, a couple of slips, and a few undershirts. She also ordered a few white socks, which all had the same style. Mommy said if I lost one, then it could be easily paired with the rest.

It seemed like everyone who was anyone had a pair of Buster Brown shoes. We shopped at the Sears department store to have my feet measured. There were many shoes to select from, but I only wanted one kind. As much as I begged for Buster Brown shoes, I didn't get them. I probably was the only one on the planet who didn't have a pair. Mommy said the shoes she picked were made equally as well as the Buster Brown shoes and cost almost half the price. They were definitely separate but far from being equal. As ugly as I thought they were, I should have been more grateful. Daddy's wages were about seventy-five cents an hour. I also wanted a pair of barrettes for my hair, but Mommy insisted on buying ribbons.

The first day at Stony Brook Elementary School was like going to a circus. I had never seen so many children in one place. I was fascinated and yet a little disappointed because none of the children looked like the ones on *Rumpus Room*.

My teacher's name was Mrs. Irving. She was the same color as the *Rumpus Room* teacher. Finally it all made sense! The reason Miss Joann never called my name was because her telescope was off limits to children of my color. There must have been about twenty students in my classroom. A few students learned quickly how to climb the classroom corporate ladder. Being the teacher's pet gave them special privileges such as sitting in front of the class, handing out class supplies, and choosing what students they wanted on their play team.

Sitting in the front of the class was less distracting than sitting in the back. I sat in the back of the class with a boy named Louie Spencer. He was a troublemaker and the worst kid in the class. Louie was always hitting and fidgeting and he compulsively exposed his family jewels.

The naughty corner was just a seat away from where Louie and I sat. If Mrs. Irving caught Louie loudly misbehaving, she would send him in the naughty corner. If he touched me and I yelled out for him to stop then she would send me to the naughty corner. Louie always had candy. The aroma smelled good but his body smelled bad. He didn't seem to mind that no one wanted what he was willing to share. One of his clown-ish tricks was to bend over while working up a wad of saliva and have it hang from his mouth. Skillfully he sucked back in before it reached the floor.

Louie was good at sabotaging my precious education. How could I learn anything with him around? Perhaps he thought his disgusting acts were captivating, but I thought they were nauseating. For the most part Mrs. Irving didn't care what he did as long as we didn't disturb the class.

It didn't take me long to learn that every child in school was put into a class of their own. The teachers' pets always got to sit somewhere in front of the class and the regulars sat some-where in the middle. And the underdogs like me and Louie sat somewhere in the back. As far as Mrs. Irving's pets were concerned, Louie was the goat and I was her sacrificial lamb. How else could Mrs. Irving teach? She needed me to be there to accompany Louie.

CHAPTER 5

PORCH LESSONS

PORCH LESSON #1

Bedtime snacks were always something to look forward to. Most of the time Winky and I were served a cup of milk with a slice of Mommy's homemade cake or a couple of cookies.

It did not matter how small a meal it was, Mommy insisted that we always pray over what we ate. She taught us to say,

God is great
God is good
And we thank Him
For our food
By His hand
We all are fed
Give us Lord
Our daily bread
In Jesus' name
Amen.

On one particular night after I had my snack, washed up for bed, and said my prayers, I was in the bed but could not go to sleep. I made several trips to the bathroom just so I could see what was on television. Also on the way to the bathroom I curiously observed what Mommy was doing while she relaxed on the sofa. Often she ate an interesting snack while sipping her tea. She never went to bed without doing the newspaper crossword puzzle.

It was a Sunday night and the Everly Brothers were on television singing my favorite song, "Wake Up Little Susie." On one of my trips to the bathroom I somehow stopped in front of the television. Without realizing it I was wiggling my body to the music and waving my hands through the air. From the corner of my eyes I caught Mommy putting on her dark-green wool coat.

"Where are you going, Mommy?"

"I am going to leave the house and I am not coming back!"

"Why?"

"I am leaving this house because you will not stay in bed!"

"I will go to bed, Mommy, please don't go! Don't leave, Mommy! Please don't go!"

Despite the fact that I pleaded, cried, and clung tightly to her coat, Mommy pinched my little hands until I let go. I am not sure what hurt the most, her leaving or the pinching; either way, I screamed.

Mommy went out of the door, onto the porch, and down the steps. Somewhere into the dark, she faded. As I looked out into the darkness, all I could see was the stars in the sky. Feeling motherless made the sky seem darker than it already was. I had nothing else more to lose, she was gone, so with all my heart I screamed my lungs out for her to come back. I was scared. It was bad enough that the *Sand-Man* was on the loose. He already had free rein to get me during the night. Now that Mommy was gone, what hope did I have?

After going back into the house, I stood in front of the television and gave the television screen a slap. I cried out to the Everly Brothers and told them to shut up! It was their fault that I was in trouble. It was their singing and their music that kept me awake. Being motherless would have never happened if I had been asleep like Little Susie.

I suppose it was my dreadful screaming that brought Mommy back to the house. When I saw her standing on the porch in front of the door, I almost collapsed.

"Are you going to be good and stay in bed?"

"Yes, Mommy, I will be good and go to bed."

My lesson for that night was to never get out of bed and dance in front of the television after I had said my nighttime prayers.

PORCH LESSON #2

There was this one summer afternoon after watching *Rumpus Room* when my brother and I chased each other all around the house. Mommy told us to find a spot and keep still because her stories were on. At that time television soap operas were only on for fifteen minutes. Mommy was heavily into watching those programs. Winky and I obeyed her for about a minute or two and then we resumed chasing each other. We were having so much fun that we did not notice Mommy's impatience.

Mommy sent me and my brother outside on the porch. Normally I loved going outside and it was always a pleasure to be on the front porch, but not during caterpillar season.

The fat, hairy worms inched their bodies all over the porch, including its ceiling. We screamed and hollered as the fuzzy creatures dropped from the ceiling of the porch. Some fell onto our heads and shoulders. I screamed and my brother cried. We tried not to step on the juicy things, but there was no place to put our feet.

We screamed in horror and frantically banged on the front door. Mommy showed a little mercy by opening the front door and handing me a broom. Actually we did not want to sweep the caterpillars away; we wanted to come inside the house.

Even if Mommy was watching her television soap operas, she could not have possibly enjoyed the television for hearing the opera that came from our mouths. Even though both of us were outside in the heat of the day, crying hysterically, I know she had to be more worried about Winky than me. His exhaustion could lead to a terrible nose bleed.

After screaming as if we were being killed by caterpillars galore, Mommy let us come back in the house. From that day on, I learned that when Mommy said to stop running through the house that was exactly what she meant.

PORCH LESSON #3

One hot summer afternoon while Winky was napping inside the house, I rested quietly on the porch. It was so hot I found the coolest side of the porch and stayed there. I fell asleep with my belly against the seat of an old wooden kitchen chair. I woke up to the sound of Sandra talking to her best friend Lee Lee. The girls stood alongside a tree with their backs facing me. They nonchalantly picked leaves from the tree while they giggled and chatted.

Shortly afterwards, they waved their arms to three other girls. I could see them getting closer as they walked through the weeds and briars. The girl in front must have caught the worst of the weeds because she rubbed her hands over her legs and ankles a little more than the other two girls. When all of the girls united they stretched their arms as if they were modeling their sundresses. Judging from the hair that grew under their armpits they were all older than me.

As they stood around in a circle, they poked each other on the shoulders while also pointing to themselves. Sandra put all that poking and pointing to an end by raising one of her arms

high in the air and making a fist with her hand. She said something to the girls while pointing one finger into the air and
then she counted to three.

"One...two...three!"

On that third count all the girls including Sandra squatted
on the ground. In my mind I wondered, *What kind of London
Bridges game is that?*

My second thought was they should be using the outhouse. As their eyes dashed from one person to the next, they
whispered and mumbled words that I could not hear. Finally
all eyes gazed upon Sandra. From the way each girl nodded, it
appeared that they had come to some neutral agreement.

Suddenly, like a jack-in-the-box, Sandra sprang to her feet;
one by one, each girl followed her and rose from where they
stooped. They straightened out the bottoms of their sundresses
by using their hands to brush their hems back down to their
knees. While they did that, Sandra tilted her head from left
to right. She also pointed her thumbs directly toward herself.
While strolling around each one of the girls, Sandra stepped
forward with one foot and dragged the other foot forward
behind her. I was not exactly sure what she was boasting about,
but I heard her say, "I told you before I had the most, but you
all did not believe me. I am the queen of you all, I am the
queen! You hear me! Ha! Ha! Ha! I am the queen!"

Other than strolling around like the queen, what other
queenly qualities did she portray? Where was her scepter and
where was her crown? I certainly did not see her jewels. Her
sundress was far from what a queen would wear.

When it was time to depart, Sandra and Lee Lee waved
good-bye to the three girls. Sandra continued to enjoy her
victorious moment as she marched backwards to watch the
other three girls walk out of sight. As Sandra marched backwards her best friend walked forward facing me.

All of a sudden Lee Lee stretched open her eyes, and with one hand she covered her mouth. At the time I did not understand her actions. Meanwhile another expression came over her face.

"Look at Mona Lisa, she is digging in her nose and eating it too! Eek!"

I felt so bad. I wanted to disappear. Mommy had talked to me before about my bad little habit, but it was not until Lee Lee embarrassed me that I realized having my finger in my nose was socially unacceptable.

After Sandra turned her body to face me, the green of her eyes connected with mine and then she looked away. "Leave her alone, Lee Lee! Come on, before she tells!" As the girls walked by the porch, Lee Lee stuck her long tongue out at my face.

This was the first time I remember anyone sticking their tongue out at me. It did not feel good to see her do that. I needed no explanation as to what it meant. The deed was self-explanatory.

I was embarrassed; they were embarrassed; we all were embarrassed. Lee Lee tried to make me look like I was the nasty one, but what about the contest she just lost? I think we all saw a little more than we had expected.

That day Sandra's queenly pride came just before her embarrassing fall. I learned that afternoon to not pick my nose publicly.

PORCH LESSON #4

It was a hot summer day, but it was even hotter inside the house due to the burning coals and wood inside the iron stove. Mommy was preparing the evening meal. While she cooked, I asked her for permission to go outside. She allowed me to play on the porch, but I was not allowed to take one step off the porch.

After playing on the porch for a while, I had the desire to put my feet in the dirt that was on the ground. In order to get to the ground I would have to leave the porch. The ground was only four stairs away. It was a combination of the dirt and the cool grass that seemed to be calling my name.

The door to the living room was open wide. Through the screen door I could hear the cooking spoons being tapped on the pots, which usually meant that Mommy was tending the stove. If she stood at the stove, then it would mean that she had a clear view of anyone going up and down the steps. If she was at the kitchen sink washing dishes, it would put her out of view of what I wanted to do.

Every now and then I peeked through the screen door to check out Mommy's whereabouts. The temptation of going down the steps and getting into the dirt was far more tempting than just staying on the porch.

While Mommy washed the dishes, I felt this was my opportunity to go for it. The gritty ground was very warm to my feet. Our steps had planks but no back boards. On the ground under the steps lay a can, and out of curiosity I picked it up. A wavy mist of smoke came from the can along with a foul-smelling odor. I am not exactly sure what it was I expected to see, but there was no genie to be found. Since I could not read the lettering on the can, I had hoped that its picture would give me some idea of what was in the can. The label on the can was red with black lettering. The face on the can was also red with black horns coming from its forehead. Its mouth was open wide with its black tongue hanging from its mouth. It appeared to be laughing at me. It eyes began to shift from left to right. I could hardly believe what I was seeing.

I threw the can down to the ground, ran up the steps into the house, and headed straight to the kitchen entrance. As I stood there, I felt as if I was going to faint. Mommy was too busy poking at the fire in the stove to notice the fear and anxiety on my face. What I had just seen was not normal. To tell her about the animations I had seen on that can would only prove that I did go off that front porch. As much as I wanted to tell her about the can I didn't because I didn't think she would believe me. Besides, in case she did, I didn't want to take the chance on hearing something I could not handle. As far as I was concerned, none of it would have happened if I had stayed on the porch. Out of all of my porch lessons I swore to myself that this was one lesson I would never tell.

THE *BOGEY-MAN*

That night after seeing the can, I washed up for bed, ate my bedtime snack, and said my nighttime prayers. Mommy stopped by my door while I prayed.

"Now I lay me down to sleep, I pray the Lord my soul to keep, if I should die..."

I could not go on any farther; there were questions I needed to ask.

"Why are you stopping?"

"Mommy, when we die, does it have to be in our sleep?"

"No, we can die any time."

"I don't want to die."

"Everyone dies sooner or later."

"I don't want to die."

"Why are you saying that?"

"Every night when I say my prayers I say, 'If I die before I wake,' and I don't want to die."

"Listen, as long as you are good, you should not have anything to worry about."

"What do you mean, as long as I am good, Mommy?"

"You remember what I told you before, if you are good, you will go to heaven. Finish saying your prayers so you can go to bed."

"If I die before I wake, I pray to the Lord my soul to take. God bless Mommy, God bless Daddy, God bless Winky, and God bless me. Amen."

Needless to say, that night Mommy's words of wisdom did not bring me much comfort. I was wrong for leaving the porch earlier that day. If God did not see me then the devil sure did. The eyes that I'd seen moving on that can felt like a warning to me. I never should have sneaked off the porch.

Every time I closed my eyes to sleep, I saw those haunting eyes that I saw moving earlier on that can. I promised myself that night that I would not shut my eyes or go to sleep until Daddy came home. I knew he was building us the house in Mulberry, but I would have felt safe if he had been with us on Pine Street that night.

I was nervous and afraid. Rather than just lying there and biting my finger nails, I comforted myself by singing the "Jesus Loves Me" song. I sang the first verse and the chorus. Before I could sing the chorus again, Mommy interrupted, "You better go to sleep!" Immediately I stopped singing out loud and sang it in my mind.

The volume of the television in the living room could be heard from my bedroom. Mommy may have been waiting for Daddy too. Every so often I could hear the sound of the newspaper crinkle as she did her daily crossword puzzle. The crinkling of the newspaper seemed to have slowed down. After the next set of commercials the newspaper crinkles had stopped. I was almost positive Mommy had fallen asleep.

In my mind I still sang that "Jesus Loves Me" song. The next television program was about to be aired. The clock music that played before the show knocked the "Jesus Loves Me" tune right out of my head. Before I knew it I was humming the clock music tune.

My heart nearly stopped when I heard Mommy say, "If you don't stop all that humming and go to sleep, the *Bogey-Man* is going to get you!"

"Mommy, who is the *Bogey-Man* supposed to be?"

"The *Bogey-Man* comes during the night to get children who don't go to sleep."

"What does he look like, Mommy?"

"I don't know. I heard he blends in with the dark. Now go to sleep before he comes to get you or I will get my belt."

If I had to choose, I think I would have rather been spanked; at least I knew how that would end. For me to be able to wake up each morning unharmed in the bed where I last went to sleep was starting to look like a miracle. I had to ask myself how many more night creatures roamed the night in search of children who did not go to sleep.

That night I tried very hard to go to sleep. Each time my eyes closed I would see a set of eyes looking right back at me. In my mind I not only saw Mommy's invisible eyes but also the moving eyes on that can and the face that went with it.

Although the television was in the living room, its light reflected shadowy silhouettes on the walls in my room. When the shadows moved, all I could do was hope that it was not the *Bogey-Man* or the *Sand-Man*. At that point I didn't see goodness and I didn't see mercy. The only thing I wanted to really see was Daddy coming home.

CHAPTER 6

LITTLE RED RIDING HOOD

It felt good to be in the first grade. No one could call me the kindergarten baby anymore. With Sandra by my side, I felt safe when I walked to and from school.

At Stony Brook Elementary School, my first-grade teacher's name was Mrs. Davis. Most of the children who were in my kindergarten class were also a part of my first-grade class, Louie Spencer included. Once again we found ourselves sitting in the back of the class. Besides being a little taller, Louie still remained the same. For attention, he still dropped his pencils on the floor, he frequently raised his hands to go to the bathroom, and he coughed clearly on purpose.

One of the things I liked best about walking to and from school was shuffling my shoes through the ocean of dried colored leaves. I could hardly wait till all the leaves fell to the ground. Autumn was already in the air and Halloween was just around the corner.

One afternoon Mommy took me to one of the local dime stores to shop for a costume. I saw the costume I wanted. I knew exactly who I wanted to be for Halloween. Mommy wanted to buy me a princess costume, but the only costume that appealed to me was Little Red Riding Hood. It came with an eye mask and a satin red hooded cape. To me that cape was all the costume I really needed.

At school, everyone dressed for the Halloween party. We sang Halloween songs, ate cupcakes, and drank juice. Most of the children wore store-bought costumes. Louie created his own costume. He wore a fake mustache drawn from an eyebrow pencil. He wore a man's dress hat that had a feather in its band. His jacket almost came down to the shoes. Judging from the size of his hat, the length of his jacket, and those size-ten shoes, Louie's costume must have belonged to his father.

I was so happy and excited about wearing my Little Red Riding Hood costume that I couldn't wait till we marched in the Halloween costume school parade. As we marched around the school Louie Spencer tried his best to turn my most glorious moments into a living nightmare. During the parade, he pestered me by poking me in my back and pulling back on my hooded cape.

"Stop pulling my hood! Louie, stop!"

"You are not Little Red Riding Hood!"

"Yes, I am!"

"You are not!"

"Yes, I am!

"You are Mona Lisa and Mona Lisa is not Little Red Riding Hood!"

I wanted to cry and at the same time hit him across his face. It wasn't long before Louie's pestering came to an end. He got caught opening his coat costume and flashing his six-year-old birthday suit. Everyone including me screamed in pandemonium. Mrs. Davis took Louie out of the parade and had him stand on the school steps alongside the principal.

While marching in the parade, someone shouted, "Hey, Lee Lee! Your brother is standing on the steps with the principal!" I had never made the connection that they were siblings. At that point, it all began to make sense, especially when Lee Lee's eyes connected with mine. Again she stuck her tongue at me. I certainly showed her that I could do the same. Who did she think she was without a Halloween costume? I was pretty sure she lost that big-girl contest by more than just a hair, and without a costume she had no business being in the Halloween school parade.

The parade was over, and the school day had ended. I waited in back of the school yard for Sandra to walk me home, but she was nowhere to be found. One of my classmates agreed to walk me halfway home. For the most part, I was still in my glory. At that time I had no idea of encountering any danger until I heard in stereo, "You are not Little Red Riding Hood! You are Mona Lisa!"

I felt trouble coming and feared what could happen next. My friend and I started walking away from the school. The faster we walked the faster they walked. They were gaining on us like wolves. Before I knew it they were upon us. First Lee Lee threw me down into a pile of dry weeds and then Louie grabbed a handful of leaves and stuffed it inside the back of my cape. My hands and my knees felt pricked from whatever was sticking into them. I screamed and cried as if my life was in real danger. My friend who offered to walk me home didn't know what to do. Although she wasn't the one being picked on, she also knew that she was no match for Lee Lee and Louie. Somehow above all my screaming and crying, I also heard the sweetest voice.

"Leave her alone, Lee Lee, and you too, Louie."

When I came up from the ground, I was horrified at the sight of all the arrow-shaped thistles that were stuck in my palms and my knees. Thistles were all over my coat, and many of them clung to my socks as if they were part of its design.

Although I was relieved that Sandra had caught up with me, I still cried. She tried to brush the thistles away with her composition book, but it was too painful to me. She managed to pick some of the thistles out of my hands and she took the leaves out from the back of my neck and my back. She held onto the hood of my costume and pulled it over my head and said, "Now you look more like Little Red Riding Hood."

For some reason, just to hear her say that made me feel a whole lot better.

SANTA CLAUS

During the Thanksgiving season Mrs. Davis taught us that the pilgrims came to America and found an abundance of turkeys and used them for food to celebrate Thanksgiving. In our classroom we celebrated Thanksgiving by using construction paper and real turkey feathers to make turkey decorations. We also made real cranberry sauce. After Louie Spencer stuck his hand in the pot, I did not want anything to do with the cranberry sauce. At the end of day the school principal came to our class dressed like a pilgrim and by his side was the real live turkey.

After the Thanksgiving holiday was over, we took down all the projects we created for Thanksgiving and started another project. It must have taken about a couple weeks to get our classroom to look like a Christmas winter wonderland. I had never seen so much construction paper, glitter, and glue. The smell of paste was all over the classroom. Louie must have thought it was cake icing by the way he licked it from the wooden popsicle stick.

For our classroom Christmas party, each student was instructed to bring a gift to exchange in the grab-bag box. Most of the gifts came from novelty dime stores. Everyone's eyes gazed upon the decorated carton displayed in the front of the classroom. Every gift in the box looked beautiful except for one. The wrapping paper was no more than a greasy brown paper bag. When it was time to pick a gift, each student seemed to be happy with the gift they chose except for the last student. Louie was exceptionally happy when he picked his. The last child to receive her gift cried because she didn't want the greasy brown paper bag that came from no one other than Louie Spencer.

Near the end of that school day a man dressed in a Santa Claus outfit visited our classroom. He carried a sack made of burlap. The sack was filled with red and white candy canes. All my classmates seemed to be very excited about this Santa Claus. He wore a red and white jester hat. His outfit was traditional. His suit was red and white. He wore white gloves. His belt and boots were black. He even had long white hair covering his head and face. His entire outfit seemed to fit the bill, but I knew that he was an imposter. Two things gave him away. He was not fat and his face was not white. His color was the same color as mine and the rest of my classmates.

Didn't my classmates know that Santa was a white man? I felt that we were cheated. I had hoped to see the real Santa so that I could tell him what I wanted for Christmas. As a matter of fact, this Santa Claus had the same voice as the principal.

Christmas was just a few days away and we still did not have a Christmas tree. What was Daddy waiting for? When he finally brought home the Christmas tree, he and Mommy decorated it with light bulbs and dressed it with angel hair. The only thing it needed was for Santa to find it.

This Christmas, my request for Santa was simple. What I wanted from Santa was to bring me another doll that cried tears like the one he gave me before. That doll couldn't be fixed. Its scalp had come apart from its forehead and face. I also wanted Santa to bring Sandra something.

This Christmas I was eager to meet Santa. This was not the *Sand-Man's* night or the *Bogey-Man's* night; this was one of the best nights of all nights. This was Santa Claus' night. For some reason on that night the *Bogey-Man* and the *Sand-Man* were of no concern to me. Although I felt peaceful, I had the hardest time trying to go to sleep.

I did not want to miss seeing Santa Claus, so I went from dashing from my bedroom window to dashing to our Christmas tree. When I looked out the window I hoped to see him and his reindeer. When I looked under the tree I hoped to see his presents. I suppose Mommy thought I had dashed one time too many. On that last dash Mommy explained that if Santa caught me awake, he would put pepper into my eyes and not leave me any toys.

"Mommy, why would Santa want to put pepper in my eyes?"

"That's what he will do if he catches you awake."

"I don't want Santa to put pepper in my eyes."

"Just go to bed. Go to sleep before Santa catches you!"

How could the most glorious night of the year become a blinding nightmare? I thought Santa was the good guy.

On Christmas morning I woke up to the smell of bacon and the aroma of coffee. To hear the sound of sizzling bacon and percolating coffee was more than music to my ears. When I heard Mommy whipping the eggs and tapping the fork against the bowl, I knew it was morning. The sizzling, the percolating, the whipping and tapping had its own orchestra, but it was Christmas!

For a moment I thought I was blind! I thought that Santa had done something to my eyes. My first instinct was to wipe my eyes, and when I did, the brightness of the morning light brought pain into my eyes, but at least they weren't burning. I was relieved when I gathered that my eyes were glued from natural sleep and not from Santa's pepper. As my eyes began to focus I raised myself from my pillow to see if any of Santa's pepper had been sprinkled, but to my delight I didn't see any such thing. Next I got out of bed and ran to the living room to see what Santa left under the tree, and then with excitement I ran back to my bedroom to get my brother Winky.

Toys were everywhere, but the one that I felt most drawn to was the doll that stood in a manufacturer-sealed box covered with cellophane. I could not believe it was the bride doll. I knew it was mine but I wanted to be sure. When Mommy came from the kitchen she confirmed that it was my doll.

In all of her glory, my doll was dressed in a beautiful white satin and lace bride's gown. I was not crazy about the straight pin that was stuck in her head, but it was there to hold her veil in place on top of her curly brunette hair. Her stockings were nylon and her shoes looked like they were made of glass.

As soon as she came out of the box, I put her to my nose. To me there was nothing like that new smell of a doll. Her moveable eyelids were able to open and close. She did not have any teeth. I pretended her mouth could move as I spoke for her. I named my bride doll Theresa and immediately we became best friends. She was responsible for bringing my doll conversations to a mature level. With Theresa there was no *ketch-ee ketch-ee koo* or *goo-goo gaga* baby talk.

After the awe of having a new bride doll simmered, I began to take noticed of my other presents. I was happy with my new tea set and Winky was content with his new set of cap guns. Daddy gave Mommy a brand-new coat and Mommy gave Daddy a brand-new pipe. After watching everyone ooh and ahh over their gifts, I look around to see what Santa left for Sandra. I had not forgotten what Daddy had said last year. He promised that as long as we lived in that house, he would make sure that Santa Claus brought Sandra a gift under our tree.

"Mommy, where is Sandra's gift?"

Reaching down to the stack of gifts left for other people, Mommy grabbed the one gift on top. She waved it through the air.

"You mean this one?"

Smiling from ear to ear I asked, "Is that for Sandra, Mommy?"

While holding the present above her head she nodded and said, "Santa Claus left this for Sandra. Do you want to give this to her?

"Mommy, can I hold it?"

"Yes, but don't shake it!"

"Why?"

"It might break."

"What's inside?"

"We will have to wait and see."

"Can you tell me? Please?"

"Santa told me not to tell anyone."

"Can I give it to Sandra?"

"Do you want to have her over for breakfast?"

To have Sandra share Christmas with us would be like giving me another gift.

Mommy picked up a box of cookies wrapped in tin foil and handed it to Daddy.

After returning from Sandra's, Daddy said, "She will be here in a few moments."

Knock! Knock! Knock!

Mommy stopped me from running to the door. Daddy asked, "Who is it?" When I heard Sandra voice, I opened the door as fast as I could. As soon as I saw her I wanted to show her my bride doll but something told me that this was her moment. Let her feel like a queen.

I hugged her as tight as I could and held her hand. I couldn't keep quiet any longer.

"Sandra! Santa Claus left a gift for you, but Mommy says not to shake it."

Mommy helped Sandra take off her coat and handed the gift to her. Sandra sat on the sofa and held her Christmas gift to her chest as if it was too precious to open. I offered to help open it, but Mommy insisted that I let Sandra open her own gift.

While she unwrapped her gift and opened the box, her eyes began to widen. There was Christmas candy inside along with a comb and brush set and a handheld mirror and a pair of styling combs to help hold her hair in place.

"Thank you, Mr. and Mrs. Cartman. I can't wait to style my hair so I can wear the combs."

The smile on Sandra's face was all the thanks I needed to see. Her face looked just as radiant as our Christmas tree. Too bad she wasn't able to smile like that all the time. Now that Sandra had her moment of glory, I wanted to share with her some of mine. When I reached for my doll, Mommy told me to show it to her later. Mommy said that we should eat while the food is hot, but I believe it was because Sandra may have been very hungry. From the moment she came in the door she could hardly keep from looking toward the kitchen.

Winky was pretty much content playing with his toys and did not want to eat. Daddy had to pick him up and put him in his high chair. Sandra sat across the table from me. She didn't take her eyes off the food that Mommy had put on her plate. When she reached for her fork, Mommy told her to wait until the food was blessed. Daddy blessed the food. While he was blessing the food, I kept my eyes on Sandra and Sandra kept her eyes on her food.

I only wished that she was as happy as I was. It was evident that her face was not washed, but that didn't really matter because no matter what, she was still beautiful. As soon as Daddy said "Amen," she unfolded her hands and grabbed her fork. Sandra ate her food as if she could not eat it fast enough.

After we ate, I showed her my bride doll. Sandra touched my nose and said, "Theresa is pretty just like you, Mona Lisa."

I always like the way Sandra said "Mona Lisa." Her voice was sweet. Lee Lee and Louie's voice always sounded like the call of a crow.

When it was time for Sandra to leave, she turned to my parents and thanked them for her gift. She glanced into the kitchen and thanked them also for the breakfast. Sandra acted like the gifts came from my parents instead of Santa. She went on to say it was the best Christmas she had had since her father died.

Before I could say another word, Daddy and Mommy wished her a merry Christmas. Other than Sandra's last comment, my Christmas was wonderful and felt complete.

CHAPTER 7

MOVING DAY

Later that winter, I hardly saw much of Daddy because every day he was in Mulberry working on our house. He said that the house was almost finished and ready for us to move in. I couldn't wait till after school to tell Sandra the good news. I thought she was going to be happy when I told her, but all of a sudden she blurted, "When your family moves, I'm leaving!"

"You mean your family is going to move upstairs when we move out?"

"No! I am going to run away!

"Run away? What do you mean, run away?"

I did not exactly know what run away meant, but I had sense enough to know that it didn't sound good.

"I'm going to leave home and never come back!"

"Why? Where will you go?"

"Listen to me, Mona Lisa, Sam is nothing like your daddy and you know it! He's not my real father and I hate him!"

"What do you mean he is not your father?"

"Sam is just my mother's boyfriend. My real father got killed."

"Killed? How did he get killed, Sandra? Who killed him?"

"Sam says my father was shot because he owed a man two dollars in a card game and didn't have it. The man wanted his money right away and shot him in the chest with a .38 pistol. Daddy died before ever reaching the hospital. It was a setup,

I know it was. When your family moves to Mulberry I'm running away!

"Sandra, what's a setup?"

"My father always had money. I think Sam stole his money. Sam used to always drop by the house when my father wasn't home. On the night my father was killed, he and Sam were at a card game. I know for a fact my daddy always had money. Sam was always borrowing money from him. You may not understand it, but Sam makes me sick and I hate him. All he does is look at me the way he looks at my mother and yet I know he can't stand me because I look very much like my father. I know it was Sam who set him up."

Sandra was right, I didn't understand everything she talked about, but I still nodded my head because it seemed like the right thing to do. All I wanted was for her to be happy like me.

"Sandra, when our family moves, then your family can move upstairs to where we live now and then maybe things will get better for you like it did for us! I never liked living in that basement."

"Mona Lisa! Are you listening? The only place we may be moving is right on the street!"

"Moving on the street? Why would your family want to move on the street?"

"Sam hardly ever has any money for rent. Your father has helped us out many times. If it wasn't for him we'd be on the street right now! Do you remember when Sam used to hit me? The only reason he stopped was because your father threaten to hurt him."

"Why did he always hit you, Sandra?"

"I told you that you wouldn't understand. Sam is a jealous man. He has always been jealous of my father. He wanted everything my father had. Come on, Mona Lisa, I don't want to talk about it anymore. I've already figured it out. When your family leaves...I'm leaving too, even if it means running away." Winter was almost over, and although the air was a little chilly, it felt like spring. It had been three years since Daddy first put the shovel to the ground of our new house. Now, right there in Mulberry stood our beautiful home. Finally the day came that we had been waiting for. It was about dinner time when Daddy walked in the house with a square piece of paper in his hand. Mommy looked excited, as if she knew what it was, but she held on to her composure.

Each time he tried to read what was written on that paper, his eyes filled with tears. I had not seen tears in Daddy's eyes since Mommy was last hospitalized and I had never seen Daddy ever at a loss for words. He proudly read that square piece of paper as if it was an excellent report card. In a sense, I guess it was one of the best reports he had ever read. Daddy was happy to announce that the inspector gave the approval for us to move in our new house. With his eyes fixed upon that paper, it was clear to see that his dream had finally come true.

That certificate of occupancy was our ticket off of Pine Street. Still, there were a few concerns about our new house that Daddy still had weighing upon his shoulders, but he carried them as if he was Mr. Atlas. What was written on that certificate gave our family a very triumphant moment and a reason to celebrate.

When Daddy was building the house, I didn't mind watching him mix the cement for the bricks that he laid. My eyes were forever blinking when he'd hit the nails with his favorite hammer. There were times the zinging sound from his electric saw refused to leave my mind, but according to our new certificate, those days were almost over. There was still some work that needed to be done, but that didn't matter because the pounding of Daddy's hammer and the zinging of his saw was always music to my ears.

On moving day, the house was filled with enthusiasm. Everything in my room was already packed. I tried to stay out of the way, but there was nothing else for me to do.

Neighbors and friends dropped in. They acted as if we were moving to another state or to some remote island. Mulberry was only five miles away.

Some people came to wish us well and others came to see if our plans were really true. For the most part I believe that the majority of them came to see what we intended to leave behind.

Out of all the people that came to visit, there was only one person I wished to see. I went from person to person to ask if they had seen her. Every answer was no. Finally I went to the person I should have asked in the first place.

Sam said that she went to Lee Lee's house. I wanted to believe him. I hoped it was true. Wishing her well was all I wanted to do, but how well could she be with a stepfather like Sam?

I couldn't see them coming, but I knew they were close. The sound of the motors and the shift of the gears told me it was my uncles driving their watermelon trucks. The rocks and gravel sounded like the makings of popcorn.

Like Paul Revere, I yelled, "They are here! They are here!"

From the moment I heard their trucks I began to jump up and down. All I needed now was just to see them. One of the trucks backfired. They sounded like gangbusters coming down Pine Street. The first truck that came into view was Uncle Jack's. The front of his truck had a square metal grill. Tied to the antenna was a raccoon tail. As I ran to the end of the yard to greet him I shouted, "Over here, Uncle Jack! Over here!"

Right behind him came Uncle Jim's truck. Both trucks looked pretty much the same to me. I couldn't wait for both of them to park so that I could hug them.

Somehow Mrs. Hawkins found out that we were moving. After renting from her for three years, Daddy didn't want to see her ever again. Nevertheless, here she came in her brand-new car. She drove right up in the yard and parked behind Uncle Jim's truck as if she could put an end to this wonderful event. Her son and daughter were also in the car.

She stepped out of her car wearing a mink hat and a mink shawl. She did look nice, but I don't think anyone was impressed by it. Her open-toe heels were beautiful except for her crow-looking feet. Mrs. Hawkins appeared to be a little nervous as she unnecessarily adjusted the mink around her humpbacked shoulders.

Daddy stood on the front steps of the porch like a king. He waited for her to come to him. As she walked with haste, she called his name.

"Mr. Cartman! Mr. Cartman!"

How strange! When did Daddy become Mr. Cartman to her? She always called him Joel.

"Joel! Oh...I'm sorry..." After clearing her throat she went on to say, "Mr. Cartman, I heard that you're moving today. I'd hate to lose you as a tenant. I saw the house in Mulberry you built and I've come to make you an offer."

Daddy looked her straight in the eyes and asked, "What kind of offer, Mrs. Hawkins?"

"If you let me buy your house, I will come down on your rent."

Daddy pointed his finger to the front door and then he responded, "Mrs. Hawkins, why would I want to sell you my house and stay here? Would you ever want to live in this house?"

He also had a few other words to say that left her mouth open and gasping for air. Whatever he said must have been shocking because she couldn't keep her gloved hands from around her neck.

Since Daddy wouldn't sell her our house, she insisted that he pay her for the last two months of rent.

"Mrs. Hawkins, how much did you say I owe?"

Mommy walked over to Daddy and said, "Why are you asking her how much you owe? We don't owe her anything."

Daddy winked an eye at Mommy and said, "I'll take care of this, Vera." He reached into his pants pocket and asked again, "How much did you say I owe?"

"You are two months behind, Joel. I wouldn't try to cheat you on a day like today."

Daddy pulled a few dollars out of his pocket and counted the money as if he was going to give it to Mrs. Hawkins and then he reached into his other pants pocket and pulled out his wallet.

"Mrs. Hawkins, I am going to give you a tip." He reached into the fold of his wallet and pulled out a few pieces of white paper. "Mrs. Hawkins, you see these slips of paper? They are my rent receipts for the last six months. How much did you say I owe you?"

Her son took a look at the receipts and confirmed that Daddy didn't owe her anything. This was our lucky day and not Mrs. Hawkins'. Everyone on the scene laughed at her. As humiliating as it must have been for her, she still walked away and drove off with the tip of her nose straight in the air.

We had moved most of our belongings on the front porch earlier that day. Some of our possessions were packed in boxes and carried outside and placed on the ground. The house was almost empty.

When it was time to load the trucks there really was not too much to consider. Nevertheless the biggest items went on Uncle Jack's truck. The first thing that went on the truck was my parents' dresser from their bedroom. It cost thirty-five dollars when Daddy purchased it. He had talked the seller down to fifteen dollars. While moving that same dresser, one of its drawers fell out. An old folded newspaper that was attached to the bottom of the drawer suddenly ripped. What was typed on that newspaper was bad news, but what was wrapped in it was good news.

FIVE HUNDRED DOLLARS!

Needless to say, Daddy felt like an instant millionaire. In the years since then I have often heard him say, "I did not find that old dresser, that old dresser found me."

Daddy says when he first bought it he did not feel so lucky because he paid fifteen dollars for that dresser and needed to keep that money for something else. As it turned out, his little investment was as good as any first prize. I had no idea how much Daddy weighed, but according to his joyful moves he looked at least twenty pounds lighter.

From the moment we got out of bed that morning, our day went from glory to glory. In the final moments of leaving Pine Street, I raised myself to my knees to look out the back window of our car. Although I felt very happy about where we were going, I also felt a little sad. It was only a little while ago that Daddy took our dog Ticky on a one-way trip, and shortly afterwards my stillborn baby brother went on one and now it was our time; but of course there wasn't anything really sad about it. I wanted so badly for Daddy to stop the car. Memories of the house, memories of the porch, and memories of Sandra flashed clear in my mind like 3D pictures from a View Master.

Looking back at that house for the last time was not easy. I was already getting homesick for Sandra. My little heart

ached to see her just one more time. I did not want to leave
"purgatory" Pine Street without ever saying good-bye to her.
She was like a big sister to me. I promised myself that I would
never forget her.

How could I forget her? Her situation was not a forget-
table one. I overheard Daddy and Mommy saying that Sam was
a no-good person and when Sandra's father died, it not only
killed something in her mother but it also killed something
in Sandra too. They also said that Sandra's mother spent the
majority of her time smoking cigarettes and staring at the wall.

I will never forget Sandra's hurt expressions and the anger
in her voice as she talked about how her mother hardly looked
at her and how she missed her daddy calling her "Baby Girl."
Who could blame her for not liking Sam? I wondered if she
meant what she said about running away from home when we
moved. Sam said that she went to Lee Lee's house.

Wherever Sandra was, my heart prayed for her safety.
I promised myself that I would have Daddy bring me back
to visit her. I promised myself that I would never forget Pine
Street. I promised myself that I would always remember that
house. Mrs. Hawkins had been a constant reminder that what
we'd lived in was not our own, nor would we ever want it to
be. To never leave Pine Street would be like living in purgatory.
However, with all the goodness we had on one side of the coin
and all the mercy on the other, we came...we stayed...and now
we were on our way.

CHAPTER 8

NEW BEGINNINGS

Daddy was the eighth of nine siblings. Eight souls were saved on Noah's Ark. A spider has eight legs. And each time its web is destroyed, it spins a new one. Eight is the number for new beginnings. Nineteen-fifty-eight was the year we moved into our home. The town of our new beginnings also held a few memories of Daddy's past.

Living in our new place brought on its own set of challenges; however, considering where we moved from, it was nothing like "purgatory" Pine Street. Daddy always had faith. He never had trouble facing challenges. Daddy liked to say, "There is always hope when you know where to look."

Finally our family was able to enjoy the fruits of Daddy's labor, time, and money invested in a house that would always be our own.

Daddy needed more money for cabinetry, appliances, and plumbing. Because of his skin color, no bank in town wanted to give him a loan. A lawyer gave Daddy the name of an out-of-town banker whose only interest was in the color green.

Mommy was so proud of her new kitchen. Her new electric range-top stove and electric oven were her pride and joy. She was not the only one thrilled about her new cabinets. Winky and I loved her double-shelf lazy Susan. Personally, I loved everything about the house. We all appreciated the fact that we now had a furnace that gave heat throughout the entire house.

The baseboard radiator in the bathroom was the coziest one to me. Our oil-burning heat benefited Winky's bronchitis better than the soot and smoke from the pot-belly wood-burning stove used on Pine Street.

Normally everyone is born with five fingers on each hand and five toes on each foot. We use our five physical senses to touch, see, hear, taste, and smell. Our head, arms, and legs make us a five-star being. Our house was the fifth house built on Circuit Street and it felt as good and graceful as a five-star hotel.

There are twelve numbers on a clock. There are twelve inches in a foot. There were twelve apostles in the Bible whose hearts were measured by one Ruler. I think it is safe to say that twelve is a divine number—after all, our new address was 12 Circuit Street.

Our concrete porch was only considered a stoop. Its steps were made of concrete and were built to the front of the porch as well as on the side. When we first moved there I'd run down one side of the steps and up the other as often as I pleased.

Being able to play in our own front yard and in our own back yard gave me a wonderful sense of newfound freedom. Three out of the five families on Circuit Street had two children. I was six months senior to the girl next door and proud to be the oldest child on our street. Being the oldest had its price, and I suppose I paid mine through that silver strand of hair that grew from the top my head.

One of the best things I liked about living on Circuit Street was its one and only street light. I didn't exactly consider it being a lighthouse, but for me that street light served as my beacon to keep away the nocturnal creatures such as the *Bogey-Man* and the *Sand-Man*.

Our street was considered a dead-end street. At the end of the street was a large area of marsh ground that grew lots of weeds, many reeds, and all kinds of tall trees. Basically it was just a swamp. None of us children in the neighborhood left our yards without permission. It seemed as if we always had to beg to play in each other's yard. The neighborhood was pretty safe except for that swamp. Living on a dead-end street wasn't that bad because it was us children playing together that brought our street to life.

My daily routine was mostly church, school, and home. Each institution carried the power to make me or break me.

The opened end of Circuit Street led into Hickory Street. To the right of Hickory led straight out of town. To the left of Hickory Street led to the places that I visited the most. Two blocks down in that same direction was a set of four railroad tracks. This was the place school fights and petty disputes were settled. Continuing on down to the next block was New Zion. It was the first African American church built in Mulberry. That was also the church that Daddy attended when he was about six years old. His family had lived in Mulberry a long time ago.

New Zion was located on the corner of Hickory Street and Maple. After crossing Maple Street, the next block down on Hickory also had a church called Trinity Baptist. The pastor at Trinity was also the preacher that had married my parents. Three houses down on the same side as Trinity was a child-friendly store called Spano's Candy Store. I could be wrong, but I think Spano's got more of the Sunday school money than the church's Sunday school class.

Lastly, on the next block down on the same side as Trinity and Spano's, was Cambridge Elementary School. This was the first school that I attended after we moved to Mulberry and also the place where Hickory Street began.

CHAPTER 9

THE BLACK AND THE WHITE

The transition from Stony Brook School to Cambridge Elementary was certainly a cultural shock. I was still in the first grade at my new school, and my new teacher became Miss Rozan. She was the same color as the television teacher Miss Joann. After Miss Rozan introduced herself to me, she politely introduced me to the class. Next, she asked the class to introduce themselves by saying their names starting from the first row of students by the classroom door.

As each student called their name, I tried to match their face with the faces I had seen on *Rumpus Room*. Watching them say their names was exciting. I felt as if I was in *Rumpus Room*. I could hardly wait to find out if they were ever on *Rumpus Room*.

After each child introduced themselves to me, I was directed to sit in the seat in the rear of the class. It felt like déjà *vu*.

As I got halfway to my designated seat, one of the Eager Beaver lookalikes chanted these words: "Monkey, monkey! You look like a monkey!"

Surely if she was the chair person for the welcome committee then that little chant meant I was not in *Rumpus Room* anymore.

I was the same height as the rest of the students, but I could feel myself shrink to each dreadful tune of the "monkey chant."

Everyone looked at me as if mud was spilled all over my face. In order to keep from crying, I convinced myself that if I could take Louie Spencer's teasing then I could endure the "monkey chant."

After the initial shock of seeing so many Eager Beavers lookalikes, I finally realized that there were two other Colored children in the classroom. It would have been nice to have gotten a friendly wave of support from those two, but instead they looked at me as if it was my turn to be tarred and feathered. One of the little brown faces belonged to a boy name Roger Ward. Judging from the way he looked at me, I could not help but wonder if he was color blind. The other little brown face belonged to Cherry Gorden. I was surprised at her because she knew who I was. I thought we were friends. She lived right next door to me and yet she looked at me as if she had never seen me.

A few of the other students stuck out their tongues at me. I could not believe the reception I was getting. The children in my classroom made fun of me as if it was their rightful duty. The last time I felt that kind of humiliation was when Lee Lee looked at me in disgust for picking at my nose. I had really hoped the children in my new class were going to be much friendlier than my former classmates at Stony Brook. I know Louie Spencer was a troublemaker, but I don't remember him looking at me the way these children looked down on me. The transition from Stony Brook School to Cambridge Elementary School was very disappointing. Louie always called me Mona Lisa, which was actually an honor compared to the "monkey chant."

Not only was the transition from one school to another a cultural difference, it was an educational difference. At Stony Brook in my old first-grade class, I was still learning how to write my upper and lower case alphabets. At Cambridge, my new first-grade class was already learning how to spell and write words. For practice we had to write our spelling words ten times each. I didn't mind writing those words, but what was written on my paper stuck better on paper than it did in my head.

Reading may have been fundamental, but it certainly was not fun for me. In Miss Rozan's class we read the Dick and Jane reading books. Each story was filled with many illustrations. Judging from each picture, I thought learning how to read was just a waste of time. What I needed to understand was that just because pictures could say a thousand words did not mean that the illustrations gave all the clues.

Math was also more advanced in Miss Rozan's class. She wrote only numbers when showing us how to add. My first-grade teacher in the other school drew pictures such as three cats or three ball alongside the number three when showing us how to add numbers. Visual effects helped me. Without the visuals, math was just "trick-bla-ometry."

Each student was seated in class as if they were singing in the choir. The "A" students sat in the front rows like the sopranos in a choir. The "B" and "C" students sat somewhere along the middle like alto singers. The "D" and "F" students sat in the back rows like bass singers.

Faithfully I copied each homework assignment from the blackboard, but that did not mean I was going to do it. When arriving home from school, doing my assignment was as far from me as the school's classroom.

Miss Rozan informed Mommy that I needed help. At first I was glad about Mommy helping me until I saw how she responded to the answers on my papers. It bothered me to see her so frustrated. As a matter of fact, sometimes it was a little scary. Mommy's idea of getting the right answers from me was by "hitting" the wrong answers out.

Unfortunately for me, the comb that Mommy used for correction was not magical enough to change my wrong answers to right answers. The only magical thing about that comb was its illusion to look like many combs while waving in the air.

One evening Mommy warned me about my frame-by-frame progress. "If you don't start learning like you are supposed to, you will end up being a dumb bunny all of your life."

Of course she did not have to say that twice. The words "dumb bunny" rang in my mind like the fire bell. Just because I didn't want to study did not mean that I did not want to learn. Who wants to be a dumb bunny all their life?

Daddy said that I could learn anything I wanted to learn. Deep down I knew he was right, but I did not know how to make it happen. At that time, getting an "A" on my paper would not have changed the way I was treated in the classroom. The children that were my color were not acknowledged like the other children when they got good grades. Our teacher did not want us to climb the classroom corporate ladder. The only thing left for someone like me to climb was the monkey bars.

Being academically challenged was not exactly my entire fault. I suppose I had a few issues such as the *Bogey-Man*, the monkey chant, and now the possibility of being a dumb bunny.

The monkey chant, dumb bunny, and the *Bogey-Man*... Oh my!

Cherry often raised her hand to every question the teacher asked. I believe Miss Rozan got a kick out of watching Cherry ache to tell her the answer. Sometimes Cherry looked to me as if she was the one with all the brains but didn't know what she looked like. Didn't she have any idea what she sounded like? Many times I found myself being embarrassed for the both of us because the "Owwe-owe-owwes" and "Ahh-ahh-ahhs" that came out of her mouth sounded just as monkeyish as the names we were called by our fellow classmates.

Cherry was very focused while she worked. She kept her eyes on the chalkboard like a horse with blinders. She didn't allow herself to be easily distracted like me. She took her class work very seriously. One day I asked her, "Why don't you look at me during class time?"

Her response was, "If I don't get straight As, my parents will spank me."

I appreciated her honesty. She was the first person who taught me not to mix business with pleasure.

At the end of the school year, the state required each student to take an academic survey test. This test was not designed for the academically challenged. The easiest thing about the test was filling in the right circles for my name. The hardest part of the test was choosing the right multiple-choice answers. The smartest thing for me to do was to let my friend Clayton help me do the choosing.

In time a few of my classmates learned to treat me as if I was human. If the others weren't picking on me then they treated me as if I was invisible. It hurt to be treated as if I was invisible, but even that was better than being called a monkey.

Roger Ward kept pretty much to himself. Since he had four brothers and two sisters, no one was foolish enough to challenge him.

Friendship with Cherry was sometimes mind-boggling. There were times when we were like the best of friends, and other times it seemed as if she hated me for no reason. Although she was a straight-A, Miss Goodie-two-shoe student, she was also on the "monkey lookalike list," which did not exactly fit the bill for becoming one of the teacher's pets.

Miss Rozan was more lukewarm than neutral. She did not promote unfairness, nor did she stop it, but I forgave her on promotion day.

CLAYTON

Since we moved to Mulberry, going to bed was not as scary as it used to be. The *Sand-Man* and *Bogey-Man* were practically obsolete. Although Mommy hardly mentioned them, it was sometimes difficult to shake the feeling that I was being watched.

Winky and I still shared the same room and the same bed. He slept at one end and I slept at the other. Each night he always fell asleep before I did. Usually he woke up earlier than I woke up just so that he could see the cartoons. I could never understand why he liked to watch the musical cartoons that spoke no words.

I found comfort in a friend that only talked to me. His name was Clayton. I guess that was the name that fit him best. Like fresh clay, I molded him and he molded me. Clayton and I were like one.

Clayton was always respectful to me. He made me feel good about myself. He gave me advice to not worry about the children in my class that didn't care for me. He said many of them wanted to be my friend but didn't know how.

Clayton was also the one who told me that there was no *Sand-Man* or *Bogey-Man*. Of course each time I looked in the mirror he was always there. I loved to hear him talk. Sometimes when his voice got a little too loud, Mommy would ask, "Who are you talking to?" Meaning no disrespect to Clayton, I would answer her and say, "Nobody!" I could never allow Mommy or anyone else to say anything disrespectful about my make-believe friend.

CHAPTER 10

THE TWENTY-THIRD PSALM

Although the "Now I lay me down to sleep" prayers were faster to say, it was also babyish. Mommy taught me to recite the Twenty-third Psalm. I always thought it was a beautiful psalm even when I did not know what it meant.

The Lord is my Shepherd; I shall not want.

He maketh me to lie down in green pastures: He leadeth me beside the still waters.

He restoreth my soul: He leadeth me in the paths of righteousness for His name's sake.

Yea, though I walk through the valley of the shadow of death I will fear no evil: for thou art with me; Thy rod and Thy staff they comfort me.

Thou preparest a table before me in the presence of mine enemies: Thou anointest my head with oil; my cup runneth over.

Surely goodness and mercy shall follow me all of the days of my life; and I will dwell in the house of the Lord forever.

"To walk through the valley of the shadow of death" was just as uncomfortable to repeat as "If I die before I wake." What child wants to think about death before going to sleep? Death was death and I did not want to die.

Considering the fourth verse, "I will fear no evil," it was a miracle that my nose did not grow when I said that line.

I thought it was my fear-given right to be afraid of the *Sand-Man* and the *Bogey-Man*.

Lastly that fourth verse, "Thy rod and Thy staff they comfort me," made me surely wish Mommy's comb and Daddy's belt brought me comfort.

Verse five, "Thou preparest a table before me in the presence of mine enemies," made me think how lucky for Winky, Daddy, and me that no matter how angry Mommy was at us, she still prepared the kitchen table with delicious meals.

As far as enemies were concerned, Mommy's advice was if someone hit me, then hit them right back; on the other hand, Daddy said if I was bothered by an enemy, I should smile and kill them with kindness.

Also in the fifth verse says, "My cup runneth over." Perhaps God didn't mind my cup running over, but Mommy sure did, especially if the milk was being wasted.

Lastly in the sixth verse, "Surely goodness and mercy shall follow me all the days of my life." Goodness was having parents. Mercy was when they didn't spank me.

"And I will dwell in the house of the Lord forever." Mommy often reminded me that I should be especially good on Sundays. She made the consequences of not making it to heaven sound like the worst place imaginable.

CHURCH

Daddy was about six years of age when his family moved from North Carolina to Mulberry. They only lived in Mulberry for three years. Having nine children and no home of their own, his parents decided to move back to North Carolina. Although they did not live long in Mulberry, Daddy's dream was to one day move back and live there. To most wealthy people, our house was not exactly a dream home, but as far as Daddy was concerned, it was the house of his dreams.

When Daddy's family lived in Mulberry, they became members of New Zion Methodist Church. New Zion was built in 1891. It was the first Negro church built in Mulberry. The church remained nostalgic. Very few upgrades had been made since Daddy was a child. Basically the structure of New Zion Church was made of wood and the outside of the church was painted white. There was no basement except for what was connected to its parsonage. The sanctuary could seat about one hundred people. My eyes seemed to never get tired of looking at the roped carvings in the pulpit's furniture. Daddy said that same pulpit furniture was there when he was a child. The benches in the pews were a bit mismatched because some of the benches were used and donated by another church in the area. Built into the wall behind the pulpit was a stained-glass window. It was donated and dedicated in loving memory to one of New Zion's deceased members.

Daddy's love for New Zion Methodist Church still kindled as it did when he was a child. When he rejoined with New Zion he instantly became a valued member. The church didn't seem to have any repairs that he couldn't fix. He mowed the church lawn, raked the leaves, and shoveled the snow. Each cold Sunday morning Daddy would get up early to make a fire for the church's pot-belly stove. After he got the fire started he'd come back home to get dressed so that he could teach Sunday school.

Mommy was also religious and stood firm to her faith. Even now I can still hear one of her favorite proclamations, "I was born a Baptist and I will die a Baptist."

Between the two Negro Baptist churches in Mulberry, there was no question about which church Mommy would be attending. Not only did the pastor of Trinity Baptist Church marry my parents, but a host of Mommy's kin folks also attended there.

The exteriors of New Zion and Trinity Baptist were built pretty much like the one Mommy taught me to form with my hands. As a child I found it amusing to intertwine my fingers to the inside of my palms while holding my thumbs side by side. My fingers represented people and my thumbs represented the doors and my index fingers pointed parallel with my thumbs to represent the steeple, and then I would say, "Here is the church, here is the steeple, open the doors and see all the people."

Going to church was not negotiable for Winky and me. Mommy and Daddy insisted upon us going also to Sunday school. Why would I not want to go to church? This was the place where people met me with open hearts and open arms. Many of my family members could be found there along with many of my friends. Besides, I couldn't wait each Sunday to see the newest run in Miss Dee's pair of old stockings. It was always amusing to see the many ways she wore her wig. I wondered if she knew when her wig was on backwards. Her mousy voice sounded like she was singing "Bringing in the cheese" instead of "Bringing in the Sheaves."

No matter how quiet the church was or what the occasion, I couldn't help but grin each time I heard Mr. Briggs' deep voice say, "Well…" When talking on the telephone, Mommy often referred to him as "Fifty" because everyone knew that he always kept a fifth of drinking alcohol under his car seat. No one really looked down on him because he always gave a generous donation of fifty dollars in the collection plate.

Winky and I went to church with Mommy. About every two or three months we visited New Zion to worship with Daddy. Both churches showed love and open arms instead of turned heads and clenched fists as I often saw at school.

Lucky for me, singing off key was not an acceptable excuse for not singing in the children's church choir. Being allowed to be a member of the children's choir was like being in heaven. This position not only allowed me to sit in one of the best seats in church but also allowed me to be in the company of people who would bring lifelong friendships. My Aunt Essie was our pianist and choir director and her daughter P.J. was one of my favorite cousins. The choir stand was also filled with other cousins and children that I went to school with. Because of the kind friendship that existed throughout the choir, our rehearsals were about as much fun as attending a party. P.J. and I both sang soprano. Unlike school, I sat with her in the front row of the choir.

As a child I wasn't exactly sure if having parents in different denominations was a plus or a minus. Unlike Cambridge Elementary School, each church provided acceptance, fellowship, and love. At church I felt like a rosebud; at school I was treated like the stem.

Every Sunday after church, our family spent the rest of the day together. Mommy always prepared a big Sunday dinner and Daddy always took our family for a ride in the car. Most of our ventures involved visiting family and friends. Winky and I always kept our fingers crossed in hopes of visiting relatives or other families that had children close to our age.

CHAPTER 11

MISS BLISS

It was my second grade school year when Winky began kindergarten. He did not seem to be as eager as I was when it came to shopping for school. That year, Mommy took us to Sears department store. Shopping in the store was more adventurous than shopping from a catalog.

The Sears catalog was great for my imagination, but to be inside the actual store was ten times better, even if we didn't buy anything. There was no catalog in the world that could give me the same satisfaction as being able to see, touch, and smell what I was able to see in that store.

Mommy made sure the shoes we tried on were a very good fit. As a child she wore a pair of ill-fitting shoes that ruined her feet. Out of all the pretty shoes in the store, she picked the ugliest shoes for me to wear, which only came in three colors, black, brown, and gray.

Other than those ugly shoes, I was happy about my new wardrobe. I had new dresses and a sweater. My brother had new shirts and pants. I had new sashes and a belt. Winky also had a new belt and a pair of suspenders.

Although Mommy told me that she did not have enough money, I begged her for a new lunch box. After she bought the lunch box I felt a little selfish. She redeemed her S & H Green Stamps in exchange for a plaid-painted metal lunch box. Mommy had had her eyes on an electric cake mixer for a long time. She had planned to purchase one with her stamps, but instead she sacrificed her wants for my wishes.

Mommy baked cakes regularly for church, school, and home. She used a manual mixer. Although it did the job, she deserved better. Each time I saw her making a cake I promised myself that I would never beg her again for anything.

NEW MONEY

It was the first day of school of my second grade year and I felt pretty optimistic. My clothes were new, my shoes were new, and my lunch box was new. My goodness, I felt like new money, but after walking into the classroom I felt trouble rising like water in a boat. My new teacher was standing by the classroom entrance. She did not give me a chance to say my name. Barely looking at me, she pointed to the seats located in the back of the room.

On the way to my seat a red-headed freckle-faced girl by the name of Emily Trout wanted to play the hokey pokey gambit game. She stuck her foot out in front of me as I walked. She tripped me; I fell. As if all of that were not good enough, she also unloosened the sash that was tied behind my dress and then she yanked on it as if I was her horse.

The children laughed, and the teacher said, "Look where you are going, Miss Cartman, and next time don't be so clumsy!" After getting up from the floor, I turned around and tried to explain that it was not my fault, but the only thing the teacher was interested in was for me to get to my seat and sit down.

Cherry and Roger were in my class again. They laughed along with the rest of the class. I don't know why those two laughed so hard; had they forgotten what color they were?

After the late bell rang, Miss Bliss closed the classroom door. She introduced herself to the class and then sat at her desk. Before taking attendance she instructed everyone to raise their hand and say "Here" at the call of our names. I couldn't help but wonder if I was in the right class because she didn't call my name. After pausing for a moment, she asked, "Did I miss anyone's name?" I raised my hand as high as I could. She barely looked at me and said, "You don't have to raise your hand, I could see you a mile away." It hurt me to hear her say that. Emily and another girl that sat in front of me turned around and poked their tongues at me as if they were somebody and I wasn't anybody.

After taking attendance, Miss Bliss passed out white lined paper. We were asked to write down our name, address, and telephone. While we wrote on our papers Miss Bliss wrote on the chalkboard. While I was writing, Emily had the audacity to ask me for one of my pencils. I didn't mean to say it as loud as I did, but I told her "No!"

At that time Miss Bliss was writing on the chalkboard and without turning around she asked, "Who is it that I hear talking?"

When no one volunteered to give that information, Miss Bliss stopped writing on the chalkboard and turned around and repeated it again. "Who is it that I hear talking?" At that point the look on her face was now transformed to a witch. In my mind I wondered, *What kind of witch is she?*

She raised her voice again and asked, "For the last time, *which* one of you is talking?"

I practically froze when I heard her say the word "which." The possibility of her being a real "witch" made me wonder if she had read my mind.

Although it was Emily who asked for my pencil and I who responded no, Emily pointed directly at me. I tried to defend by explaining that Emily had asked me for my pencil. With no regards to my defense, Miss Bliss pointed at me and shouted, "If you talk again I am sending you into the hall!"

When the teacher turned her back, Emily reached over my desk and snatched my pencil from my hand. I told her to give it back and that was when Miss Bliss turned around and accused me of making all the commotion. For that I was sent out of the classroom and ordered to stand in the hall.

Even though it has been said that pride comes before the fall, I am positive I did not deserve the way I was treated by Miss Bliss, and I sure did not deserve the way I was treated by Emily Trout. Before I came to class that day I felt like new money. After the end of that school day I felt like less than a penny.

Our class sometimes played an indoor game called Duck, Duck, Goose. Someone was picked to be the tagger. Everyone else was sitting ducks. The game was sort of tricky. Whoever the tagger tagged to be a duck remained a sitting duck, but whoever the tagger tagged to be the goose would be the one to chase the tagger. Well...boo hoo hoo! I was never tagged to be the duck and I was never tagged to be the goose. By all means, Mommy wanted me to be different than everyone else, but I think I would have felt better about myself if she had said, "If you want to fly with the eagles then don't sit with the ducks!"

Cherry had poor eyesight. Even with her eyeglasses she still needed to sit closer to the chalkboard. I was surprised that Miss Bliss had any sympathy for Cherry because the colored students always sat in the back of the class. Being the "A" student that she was blended well with Miss Bliss's seating arrangement. Cherry acted as if it was her studious grades that promoted her to the front row seat, but in reality it was just her squinting eyes.

When it was test-taking time, the "A" students had it made. The "B" and "C" students did not really trust one another, but they did what they had to do in order to maintain their grades. I believe it was the "D" and "F" students that were the most honest. Why copy another person's wrong answer when your guess was as good as theirs?

VALENTINE'S DAY

For some people, Valentine's Day should be every day. This was the only day of the year that Miss Bliss and her little angels kept their little horns tucked neatly inside their heads.

Our class celebrated Valentine's Day by bringing in Valentine's Day candy and cupcakes and making decorations. After we ate the treats, we exchanged Valentine cards. Truthfully speaking, I was more excited about the Valentine's Day cards than the cupcakes and candy.

After everyone exchanged cards I sat in my seat and held all of the cards that were given to me as if they were one million dollars. I felt honored. I almost felt loved. Each card was real and tangible. I had never seen my name written so many times by so many people. I counted all the envelopes before I opened them.

Including myself, there were thirty-two students. I counted thirty-one cards. I didn't feel bad about the one missing card. Roger Ward's religion did not allow him to exchange holiday cards. Regardless of what we were told, I gave him a Valentine's Day card. My heart could not help it. I knew what it felt like to be left out.

When I handed Roger the card, he looked around the classroom to see if anyone was watching. Only one half of his face smiled as he laid the card on top of his desk. After giving him the card, I hunched my shoulders and walked away. After counting all my envelopes, I looked around the classroom. I guess the temptation was too great for Roger; he began reading the card that I gave him. His half smile was now one big grin.

I was happy to see that Miss Bliss was eating one of the cupcakes that Mommy had made. While she ate it, I had hoped to make contact with her eyes, but she never looked my way. I suppose I should have been happy about that. Just because she accepted Mommy's cupcake did not mean she had to accept me.

If Valentine's Day could keep Miss Bliss from riding on her broom then Valentine's Day should be every day.

RELIGIOUS DAY

Each Friday at school, I was often filled with mixed feelings. No doubt I was happy that it was the last day of school for the week, but it was also test day. Taking any kind of academic test always made my brain freeze.

Other than Fridays being test day, it was also religious day. Although I sometimes carried my rabbit's foot, it didn't take the place of having a symbol to represent having a religion.

The majority of the class came from two religious groups. One religion wore crosses around their necks and the other religious group required the boys to wear a cap call a yarmulke. Most of the class referred to that little cap as being a beanie. And the girls from that same group wore a six-pointed star with a chain around their necks. On that day, neither religion ate red meat.

Needless to say, I felt left out. For the sake of not looking heathenish, I too wanted to wear a necklace.

One Saturday morning while Mommy was straightening my hair with the hot iron comb, I asked her if she could buy me a necklace with a cross on it. Her response was, "You don't need that kind of necklace. Why do you want to wear a cross around your neck?"

"Mommy, all the Christians in my class wear crosses around their necks and I want to wear one too."

"If they jump off a bridge are you going to jump too?"

"No, but I still want a necklace like they have, Mommy."

"I told you before, you don't need a cross. What makes you holy is what you have in your heart. If you want to look holy, you better make sure you are wearing your gospel shoes. All God's children have shoes."

From the way Mommy yanked that hot comb through my hair, it was a wonder that I had any hair left to straighten. My lesson for that day was not to talk controversial matters when getting my hair straightened.

At least I was not the only child that did not wear a religious symbol. Cherry and Roger also wore none. Perhaps Mommy was right about those religious symbols. Emily Trout wore a cross around her neck and that did not necessarily keep her little horns from sticking out of her head. I thought about not offending anyone by not eating meat at school on Fridays, but that small flame of consideration went out very quickly when I thought about how everyone in the classroom normally treated me. While they ate their gefilte fish, peanut butter, and tuna sandwiches, I savored each bite of my salami sandwiches.

It seemed to me that Miss Bliss forgot that we had similar backgrounds; her forefathers had a Moses who crossed the Red Sea. My forefathers had a Moses too: her name was Harriet Tubman and she had an underground railroad.

On January 1, 1863, President Abraham Lincoln helped this country to have a civilized happy New Year. He may not have parted the Red Sea, but he parted an ocean of slavery. This miracle was called the Emancipation Proclamation. There is a tunnel that was built under a large body of water in New York

City, and that tunnel was also named after him. It is through that tunnel that all transportation coming and going to New York gets to ride on dry land.

It has been said that freedom often comes with a price. I sometimes wondered how much Miss Bliss thought I owed. Consequently, for her to have accepted my freedom, I would have needed more than just a set of signed and sealed freedom papers.

TROOPERS

The scout club was the melting pot for all religious groups and ethnic groups. Boy, I sure envied my classmates on scout day. Almost everyone in my class was a member of a troop.

On scout day, the little troopers wore their scout hats, uniforms, and special pinned buttons. They looked like dignitaries and I wanted to be dressed like them.

I was so sure that Mommy would have no objections to me joining the scouts; after all, Daddy was a scout when he was a little boy. When I asked for her permission to join the scouts nothing could have prepared me for her response:

"No!"

"Why?"

"You don't need to be a scout."

"Mommy, almost everyone in my class is a scout, even Cherry."

"So! Between you and Cherry, who is the copy cat and who is the carbon paper?"

"We are neither one, Mommy."

"Well then, don't worry about trying to be like everyone else."

"Mommy, I'd like to join the scouts so that the children in my class will like me and I want to also go on camping trips with them."

"The only trip you need to take is the one in front of the mirror. If they don't like you now, what makes you think they will like you later? You need to start acting like you like yourself."

What Mommy did not understand was that I felt left out, and it seemed to me that if I was a scout, then everyone would have to accept me and I would be the same as them.

When Cherry Gorden became a scout she did not talk to me on troop day. I had no idea a uniform could make a person change like that. On one particular uniform day she walked past me and stepped on my shoe and told me that I was black and ugly.

When she did that, I couldn't wait till I got home to tell Mommy. Mommy said, "Now that is what you call the pot calling the tea kettle black."

Mommy suggested that next time Cherry or anyone else called me names I should say, "Sticks and stones may break my bones but names will never hurt me."

All I could say about that was, "It's a good thing I'm not Pinocchio."

Daddy told me not to let her get the best of me. He advised that I should just smile and be nice when I was offended. He also said, "Sometimes you have to be like a brake shoe to a wheel. Sparks fly when two pieces of metal get rubbed together. The padded material on the brake is called the brake shoe. Without the pad the brake cannot do its job."

He said if I played the part of the brake shoe, then I could kill my enemies with kindness.

Daddy talked about "brake shoes" and Mommy talked about "gospel shoes." My friend Clayton asked me, "How does

anyone expect you to smile when you're getting stepped on
with Cherry's shoes?"

THE PROJECT

At the end of the school year each student was assigned to
do a project. For this particular project everyone was given a
partner. These projects counted as a part of our passing grade.
I was pretty sure that Cherry and I were going to be partners,
but as Miss Bliss would have it, she let the "A" and "B" students
pick their own partners. For the rest of us, we were on our
own. I don't know why I was so surprised that Cherry picked
someone else besides me. I couldn't imagine having someone
else as a partner. No one picked Emily and no one picked me.

Our projects had to be worked on outside the classroom.
I did not want Emily Trout as a partner and I certainly didn't
want her to come to my house, but I did not have a choice. It
was either that or we failed the project.

Emily could not be still. The materials for our project
were on the dining room table but she wasn't interested in
that. She ran all over the house like a little puppy. Mommy
gave Emily a warning that if she did not be still and sit at the
table, she would have to leave. Finally Emily settled down.
We made a wagon train from an oatmeal box. For the back-
ground we used oak-tag poster board. Our project turned out
to be a disaster. The horse we drew on the poster board was
hardly identifiable. The sky and ground were almost joined
and practically the same color. I was hardly amused at the way
she continually crashed the wagon train into the palm of her
hand. The glue and paste made the project look even worse.
When the project was complete, I walked her almost all the
way back to the school. On the way home I couldn't help but

wonder if putting Emily and me together was just a setup for both of us to fail.

When I got back home Mommy was waiting for me by the door. As soon as I came in the house she gave me a speech. She was talking and panting so fast I could hardly understand a word she said. But one thing was sure: I understood that she did not want me to bring Emily Trout back to our house ever again. As a matter of fact, Mommy made it clear that if I ever brought Emily to our house again then she would spank me until she got tired.

What Emily and I learned together that year probably wouldn't have filled the first chapter of a history book. I believe I sat outside that classroom more than I sat inside the classroom. The memories of Miss Bliss certainly took up a lot of space in my mind. I didn't like thinking about her. Like a negative film that faded in the sunlight, I wanted the hurtful memories of her to do the same.

Some people say that seven is a lucky number. I was seven years old when I was a student in Miss Bliss's class. I never felt lucky having her for a teacher, but I did feel lucky when she passed me to the next grade.

CHAPTER 12

SEE YOU LATER, SPECTATOR

I was seven and a half years old when I first witnessed a pool baptism. The pool was located inside our church under the floor of the pulpit. The water came up to the reverend's waist and looked deep enough to drown in. I could hardly wait till church was over so that I could ask Mommy about the pool and why those people were getting baptized. I had tons of questions. From the way those candidates shivered, the water must have been ice cold. While the ceremony was going on, the church sang "Wade in the Water." That song was sung as if the candidates were getting a death sentence.

After Sunday service, I couldn't wait till Mommy finished socializing with her family and friends. On the way to the car I anxiously asked her about that baptizing business.

"Mommy, why did those people get baptized? Do I have to get baptized? How deep is that water in the pool?"

"Just wait till we get in the car. I can only answer one question at a time."

"Winky! Did you see how deep that water was? Are you going to get baptized? I don't want to get baptized!"

Winky just shook his head from left to right. I guess I was talking too fast for him. Just to think about all that water and the song they sang made my head spin.

Until that day, I had no idea that there was a pool under the pulpit. Over and over I saw in my mind how the pulpit furniture was taken down for the baptismal ceremony. The Bible, the hymn books, and the pulpit lamp were removed. The carpet from the pulpit was rolled back and put aside. The boards of the pulpit floor were removed, and a large mirror was placed along the pool so that the congregation could witness the ceremony. The candidates looked nervous. I could hardly tell if they were freezing or if they were scared.

After we got in the car I asked, "Mommy, were you ever baptized?"

"Yes."

"How many times were you baptized?"

"You only need to be baptized one time."

"Why do people get baptized?"

"They get baptized because they have accepted Jesus as their Savior. It's customary in the Baptist church that people who want to join the church get baptized."

"Why is getting baptized customary?"

"Being baptized is a way of claiming to the world that you have accepted Christ as your Savior. It's a way of being born again."

"Savior, what's a Savior? Born again? How can that happen?"

"No more questions. Wait till we get home and then I'll explain it to you better."

For the rest of the ride home I couldn't help but wonder what Mommy meant by being born again. I didn't recall the first time I was born, and if I got baptized and drowned, I might not have remembered the second time being born. I did not want to end up being a stillborn Christian.

As soon as we got home and in the house, I asked Mommy again, "What does it mean to be born again?"

She explained, "Being born again means giving your life over to Jesus so that He can be your Savior. You don't have to worry about that until you're twelve years old. All children go to heaven, but when they turn twelve, they need to make a decision about getting baptized and accepting Jesus as their Savior because if they don't they may not make it to heaven."

At that point I was satisfied about waiting until I turned twelve years old to get baptized.

"Mommy, I believe in Jesus, but I don't want to get baptized in that pool."

"Where do you want to get baptized, in a river?"

"I don't want to get baptized in a river. Why would I want to get baptized in a river, Mommy?"

"Back home in Georgia when I was a little girl, there was no pool in our church. We got baptized in the river."

"Were you scared when you got baptized, Mommy?"

"I was a little nervous."

"Mommy, how old were you when you got baptized?

"I was almost ten years old."

"How deep was that water in that pool of our church?"

"The water was a little over three feet."

I will never forget the Sunday morning when the invitation to the church was opened. The choir and congregation sang "Come to Jesus." My favorite cousin P.J. and a few other children walked to the altar. They had never told me about their plan to get baptized. As they stood before the altar, the congregation clapped their hands as if they were all five-star athletes. Not only was I too scared to join them, I also felt a little left out.

I kept my shoes planted where I stood. I was only seven and a half years old. Mommy had already said if I died before I was twelve, I would go to heaven. I certainly didn't want to rush it by getting drowned while getting baptized.

On the day they were baptized, it seemed as if they had been given open passes to get into heaven. Although Mommy said I had until I was twelve years old, I still felt left out.

After church, when I met with P.J., she was already sharing her experience with the others who were baptized. They were all talking a mile a minute and at the same time. P.J. talked about how cold the water was, and the others talked about how they thought they were drowning. As they shared their dramatic experiences of being baptized, I had to admit that I was a little jealous. Rightfully, this was their moment. I did not mind hearing everything they had to say because I too one day planned to be a pro just like them.

The following Communion Sunday, the congregation gave my cousin P.J. and the rest of her baptized buddies the right hand of fellowship. I was just a spectator. My eyes were on P.J. through the entire little ceremony. I wanted to know what to do when it was my turn.

At home Winky and I played church. We made a podium out of the bench that Daddy made for me to stand on. I could hardly make up my mind. I wanted to be the preacher as well as part of the congregation that said Amen. Since I couldn't be both, I'd let him preach until I got tired of listening to him. Then I would tell him that I wanted to preach. If he didn't let me, then I would push him out of the way and preached till my heart's content.

One Sunday morning while the church sang the hymn "Softly and Tenderly Jesus Is Calling," I truly felt that Jesus was calling me. Between the feeling that Jesus was calling and the pressure of not being baptized like my peers, I wasn't going to risk the chance of getting left behind again. I tried to get Winky to come with me, but he would not come. I finally walked to the altar and Mommy walked up there with me. This was my moment to be welcomed. Standing there was a little overwhelming, but what worries did I have when Mommy was standing there by my side?

BAPTISMAL DAY

On baptismal day a whole lot of "what ifs" ran up and down the staircase of my mind. Anxiously I wondered *What if my foot slips off the ladder? What if I slip from Reverend Foster's hand? What if I drown? What if? What if? What if?*

All of us candidates sat on the front bench dressed in our ceremonial robes. I was nervous. As I sat there I couldn't help but turn around so that I could find my parents. After I waved to them my eyes searched for my cousin P.J. Sitting with her mom, she was not too far behind me. When P.J.'s eyes met mine we instantly waved at each other. Her encouraging smile and wave was perhaps a little more animated than mine.

I felt fine until the musician played that "Wade in the Water" music. That was the melody that indicated my time was near. Listening to Mr. Briggs made me feel a bit uneasy; he must have said "Well..." about one hundred times that morning. As I watched the others being baptized before me, it bought me time to rehearse in my mind how I was going to stand in the water and hold my breath.

When my turn came to get baptized, I was nervous. My heart pounded so hard it hurt. Inwardly I was in a panic and each footstep I made to get to the pool was just as agonizing as walking on the plank of a pirate ship.

The ladder that went down into the pool looked like it had seen better days. I did not care how many splinters that ladder had to offer, I held on to it for dear life.

The pastor and missionaries urged me to step onto the ladder. It took all the courage I had to put my foot on it. I don't remember being that cold but my teeth chattered and my body shivered. I was nervous and felt a chill, but not cold enough for my hands to freeze! My hands were frozen to that old, rugged ladder. Fear had taken hold of both of my hands like someone with a death grip. I guess I was holding up the show. The assisting deacon skillfully pried my fingers from the ladder. I was pretty sure that all eyes were fixed upon me, but that was the least of my concerns. It felt like I was in a horror movie! The shocking sensation of the water, the depth of the pool, and the somberness of that song "Wade in the Water" was more than enough to make me feel that my little life was about to come to a fearful end.

When my feet reached the bottom of the pool, Reverend Foster had to coach me into letting go of that last hold I had on that ladder. Not only was he firm with his voice, but he was also firm with his hold. His reassuring grip made it simpler for me to follow him to the center of the pool.

As we stood in the middle of the pool, Reverend Foster asked, "Dear child, what is your name?"

How was I supposed to talk with my teeth chattering like a set of castanets?

"Momomo."

Lest the ceremony be hindered, Reverend Foster said my name, "Mona Faye Cartman, I now baptize you in the name of the Father, Son, and the Holy Spirit."

After I pinched my nostrils together, down I went. My feet went from under me. I almost panicked, but before I could holler, it was over.

I was soaked. All I wanted to do now was get back to that ladder and out of that pool. I was grateful to receive Reverend Foster's aid. My robe was drenched. The weight of the water made it feel like a ton. Regardless of how it felt, I was determined to get out of that pool.

Before I could reach the top of the ladder the missionaries were reaching down to me. Their job was to wipe my face and lead me back to the dressing room. I don't mean to sound cynical, but it felt like I was being suffocated by their towels!

Of course the missionaries were only doing their job, but being able to breathe came easier after they gave their towels to me. Having my feet on the floor was a glorious moment. Not only were my what-ifs washed away, but my sins were washed away too. I was a newborn soul.

The towels weren't the only things that were around my head. It was recorded that I was baptized at the age of eight and as I said before, eight is the number for new beginnings. At that time I may have been the last one of my church peers to get baptized, which made me comparable to the eight ball in a billiard game; as long as I was in God's pocket, how could I ever lose? The towel felt good around my head but not as good as my imaginary heavenly halo.

CHAPTER 13

HOSPITALITY

Shortly after I turned eight years old Mommy began to experience pain and swelling in her upper jaw. After being X-rayed, the doctor diagnosed her with having a stone inside one of her glands. His final prognosis was that she must have that stone removed from the side of her face.

Judging from her swelling and the pain, I knew that she was going to need some kind of hospitalization. Her operation was serious; it also left me feeling a little anxious. It was only four years ago that she was fighting for her life while trying to give birth in that same hospital. I couldn't stand the possibility of her having to fight for life and me getting left behind.

Although Mommy's operation was a success, I still prayed to God every night that He would heal her so that she could come home and take care of us again.

During the time that Mommy was away, I had a little talk with my brother. Since I was older than he was, I felt that it was only natural that he should listen to me. Our little conversation turned into a dispute.

"Winky, while Mommy is in the hospital, I'm going to be your boss."

"No, you're not! You are not my boss, Mona Fay!"

"Yes, I am! I am older than you and you have to listen to me! I am your boss!"

I am sure it was the escalation of our voices that drew Daddy away from his work bench and up the basement steps. I wasn't too concerned about hearing him come up the steps because, being that I was the oldest, I thought I had the winning argument.

Apparently Daddy had heard everything we said and did not care if I was the oldest or not because he stood between Winky and me, and with his finger he pointed at both of us with a firm look on his face and said, "Listen! I don't want the two of you arguing about who is the boss! If anyone is the boss, it's me! If you don't believe me, I can get my belt and show both of you who the boss is!"

I looked at Winky, and Winky looked at me. Lest we fan the flames that came from his eyes, we both held our breaths and didn't say a word. After Daddy returned to his work bench, I respectfully said to my brother, "Okay! I won't be your boss, but I will tell you what to do."

Without any further problems he agreed. For the next two weeks that Mommy was in the hospital, I did a little soul searching for myself. I saw my mother as a tree and I as one of her branches. Although Daddy had proved that he could take care of me when Mommy was in the hospital, I still could not imagine living without her. I thought that if she died then I would die with her. I accepted that idea and felt at peace as long as Mommy and I died together.

After Mommy came home from the hospital and got a little stronger, I decided to share with her what I truly believed.

"Mommy, if you ever die, I'm going to die also."

"No, you are not."

"Yes, I am."

"You are not going to die when I die! What makes you think you are?"

I tried my best to explain the automatic process, but to my surprise she laughed and said, "You will live without me. You just can't die automatically if I die. If anything happens to me, you will still live and be all right."

I felt myself getting sick to the stomach. What she told me did not confirm what I had hoped to hear. At that point I wanted to die right then and there.

For the remainder of that day I stayed in bed. What hope did I have if she died before me? That night when I went to sleep I didn't care if I woke up or not.

WITCHFUL THINKING

On the night I told Mommy that I would die if she died, the strangest thing happened to me. When I went to bed that night I thought that I did die.

After falling asleep I tried to get out of bed but couldn't. I struggled to move, but it was impossible. I wanted to scream, but it was useless. The pounding of my heart was my only indication that I was still alive.

It felt as if my mind was awake and my body was asleep. The more I tried to move the longer the spell lasted. Why couldn't I move? Why couldn't I scream? I was so scared.

I tried to concentrate on making my fingers move. My eyes were partly opened, but I couldn't move them either. What I saw was the silhouette of the blanket on my bed.

The sound of the crickets seemed louder than ever before. I could also hear the voices coming from the television. I tried to scream, holler, and moan, but my voice was completely mute. As much as I fought to scream and move, it was all to no avail.

From the corner of my eye, I could see part of my closet door. Although I couldn't see anyone, it felt as if someone was presently there. My first thought was that it must be the *Bogey-Man*. My second thought was the *Sand-Man*. By now it didn't matter which one, because whichever it was had come from the land of "I am going to get you!" My imagination also told me that who or whatever it was that stood in my closet was also initially responsible for causing me not to be able to move.

Finally my mobility returned, but I was too tired to get out of bed. The strain of trying to move had exhausted me to the point that I no longer had the strength to move until I thought about what was standing at my closet door. Just as I positioned my arms to get out of bed, my body slipped right back into the spell.

In all my imaginations, I could not imagine what was happening to me. I had lost all my strength during that first attack and had no strength for the second one. Again, the more I fought against it, the longer it persisted. The attack seemed like eternity because I had no way of measuring time.

When the spell was finally over, I was even more physically drained than before. I was also very much afraid. In spite of being totally exhausted, I forced myself to get out of that bed so I could find Mommy and tell her about what I had just experienced.

She was in the living room sitting on the couch. The television was on. She was sipping her tea and writing in the squares of her crossword puzzle. As I stood before her wiping the sleep out of my eyes, I described to her the frightening and paralyzing experience that had just occurred. While listening she gave me such a dreadful look as if to say she couldn't believe her ears. She shook her head from left to right and then rubbed her hand and her fingers across her face and over her mouth. After taking in a deep breath she said, "Oh Lord, I prayed that you would never get it. It looks like you got it just like me."

"Got what, Mommy?"

"Well, the folks back home refer to it as an old wives' tale. They say when that happens, the *Witch* is riding you."

"Old wives' tale, what is that?"

"Oh...it's just old sayings people say that are not necessarily true. Child...all those old wives' tales and superstitions I grew up under are one of the reasons I left the South."

"Mommy, what is the *Witch*? I didn't see any witch, but it felt like something was in my bedroom and it made me so I couldn't move."

"Well...back home we call it the *Witch*."

"Mommy, what does it look like and why do they call it the *Witch*?"

"I don't know why they call it the *Witch*, but that's what they call it."

"Mommy, is it a real witch?"

"I don't know what that thing is; all I know is that they say it's the *Witch* that rides you when you're asleep."

"Mommy, after it happened to me, it happened to me again! I couldn't move and I was so scared. What should I do if it happens again?"

"Call on Jesus, just say His name when that happens and force yourself to get up, and when you do get up, get a drink of water."

"Jesus?"

"Yes, all you have to do is say His name."

"What will Jesus do?"

"He will make it stop."

I really wanted to believe Mommy, but I don't think I did. How could Jesus help me? I thought Jesus could only see me in the light and that after I said my prayers and turned off the light, I was on my own. In the light was Jesus and in the dark were the *Bogey-Man*, the *Sand-Man*, and now the *Witch*. I could not imagine why this thing was attacking me.

Okay, granted I did have a death wish before I went to bed that night, but to be *Witch*-ridden in the process made death less appealing to my soul. I was still eight years old. I thought I was at the safe age of heaven's requirements. Where was my angel when that happened? I felt I was cursed. Mommy said she was familiar with it, so could the *Witch* be a hereditary thing? Either way, I felt doomed!

Mommy called it the *Witch*. She told me what to say when it happened again but gave me no advice on how to avoid it. If I couldn't call Mommy during that "spell," then how was I going to be able to call Jesus?

CHAPTER 14

SECOND TIME AROUND

Although I did not care too much for school, I still looked forward to going to the third grade. On that first day of school, I was a little eager about attending my third grade class. Mommy had bought me a blue dress with a sailor collar from the Sears department store. I was proud of my dress and I felt it would make me look as good as any other child at my school.

When I arrived at school, I went to the back of the building. I was just as excited as all of the other third- and fourth-grade children in the school yard. A few minutes before the bell rang one of the teachers stood on the steps of the school and blew a whistle. She waited till we became quiet so that she could make an announcement.

"There are some changes that have been made. Because of the overflow of students, some of you will be going to room six."

When she called my name a sick feeling came over me. I had been in room six last year. I did not want to be in there again. I tried to comfort myself by keeping one positive thought. At least I would have a different teacher.

All of the students that had to go to room six felt humiliated because that room was where the first- and second-graders were located. We could hardly believe our ears. We felt cheated, tricked, and betrayed because we knew who taught in that classroom last year.

Knowing where we were going made the first ring of the school bell sound like the ring of doom. Already I had a bad feeling in my stomach. I was now only two classrooms away and I didn't want to go any farther. The looks on the faces of the other students told me what I already knew. I felt as if I was going to purgatory.

Miss Bliss must have sensed that I was outside her classroom door because she came to the door and signaled for me to come in.

"Come on in! You are in the right class and I am your third-grade teacher!"

Perhaps teaching the third grade was an upgrade for her, but for me it felt as if I had never been promoted. *Déjà vu*. Having her as my teacher and me for her student was no doubt a punishment for the both of us. Without waiting to be told I headed for the seat that I sat in last year.

"Where are you going, Miss Cartman?"

Instantly I stopped walking and turned around. I stood there and waited for her to appoint me to my new seat but instead all she did was flick her wrist and turn her head as if she couldn't stand the sight of me.

Emily Trout's seat was right next to mine. Everyone in class seemed to know their rightful positions. Miss Bliss hated disruptions. Everyone knew that silence was her golden rule. Her pets were the only ones allowed to break that rule.

For the next few months, everything remained the same about Miss Bliss and everything remained the same about me. My reading and comprehension was still next to nothing. When it came to math it was like learning "trick-bla-ometry." I was good about copying my homework assignments, but that didn't mean I was going to do them. Up till now my academic skills had not been complementary to any of my report cards.

At night my sleep was often disturbed by the *Witch*. At school I could hardly stay awake. I was lucky when I fell asleep in class. Miss Bliss didn't ride me and neither did the *Witch*.

Emily and I lived somewhat parallel lives. When I was four years of age my mother almost lost her life giving birth, and when Emily was four years old her mother not only lost her baby while giving birth but her life was also lost.

Emily bit her fingernails and I bit mine. We both were left-handed. Our hairlines across our foreheads were lower than most of the children in our classroom. I was self-conscious about my forehead, but I don't think she thought anything about hers. Once while I was at Trinity Baptist Church, I over-heard some choir members discussing IQs. I heard them say that people with high foreheads were much more intelligent than people with lower foreheads. After learning that new piece of information I did not want to look like I was not smart. I covered all my telltale signs by keeping my forehead covered with my hair curled into bangs.

Emily's red hair came past her shoulders. To keep her hair from falling in her eyes and all about her face, she always wore a hair band. Sometimes she wore her plastic horseshoe-shaped hair band and sometimes she wore her cloth hair bands that went around the whole circumference of her head. Emily could not have known what I knew because she did not mind ex-posing her forehead.

At the end of the year Miss Bliss assigned everyone to a project. She insisted that we work in pairs. I believe Miss Bliss had a plan to fail Emily and me by putting us together. As sure as one and one are two, I was pretty sure she knew that Emily and I together would make a zero.

Emily was very happy to have me as her partner. I only wished I felt the same. Mommy had been absolutely adamant about what she would do if I ever bought Emily to our home again. As obstinate as Mommy was about Emily coming to our house, Miss Bliss was also the same because she wouldn't give me another partner for the project. I felt as if all the odds were stacked against me. The forecast of having Emily for a partner didn't look good. I needed a miracle, because this second time around was only going to be worse than the first.

Before I brought Emily into the house, I made her promise to be still. I made her promise not to scribble all over our oak-tag paper and I made her also promise not to ask my mother for anything.

Emily and I were assigned to draw a map outline of the state of Texas illustrating the locations of its natural resources. I drew the cattle and Emily drew the oil. When we finished our project our map looked like a natural disaster.

What did it all matter? This project was already marked. Emily had been pushed on me, and judging by the way Mommy looked at her it was time to get Emily pushed to the door.

She claimed that she didn't remember how to get home. Mommy didn't like it, but she let me walk Emily to Maple Street. After watching her safely cross the street, I walked back home. I prayed each step of the way that Mommy would understand that I had no choice in the matter. I promised myself that this project with Emily Trout would definitely be the last one.

When I came in the house, Mommy's face did not seem to be quite as anxious as it was when I left. As a matter of fact, she seemed quite calm. Dinner was almost ready and Daddy would soon be home from work.

After dinner Mommy told me she had a surprise for me. I couldn't imagine what it was. It wasn't my birthday or any other special occasion that I could think of.

"What is it, Mommy?"

"You'll have to wait till bedtime."

"Is it a toy?"

"No."

"Is it something to eat?"

"I'm not going to tell you, you probably already know what it is. You may as well stop guessing because I'm not playing guessing games. Like I said, you'll have to wait until tonight."

Right before bedtime Mommy offered me a piece of cake. After I ate it she told me to get ready for bed. I knew what her surprise was when she told me to strip down to my undershirt and underpants.

I don't know why I didn't see it coming. The writing was on the wall. A year had passed since Mommy warned me. I knew that I was in for the spanking of my life because she had made a promise that if I ever again brought Emily home she would whip me till she got tired. I believe that was the only promise I ever heard Mommy make. Of course I would have forgiven her if she had broken that promise, but I guess the real thing that needed to be broken was my disobedience. Although Emily and I learned how to be friends, I also learned that obedience is always better than sacrifice.

CHAPTER 15

RAILROAD CROSSINGS

Our family car was thirty years old; it was like an old family member. For the last eight years it was the only car our family had. Not only was the car outdated, it had definitely seen better days. Each week the car seemed to be in need of some new repair. That automobile was a perfect example of what happens when fresh wine is put into old wine skins.

Daddy knew that car the way he knew the back of his hand. The only thing he didn't know was when it would break down. Mommy hated the smell of axle grease and motor oil. As far as I was concerned, the smell of axle grease and motor oil was only natural. Daddy had fingerprints on the walls throughout the house. It bothered Mommy, but it didn't bother me.

Mommy did not find anything amusing about seeing anyone's fingerprints on the doors or on the walls. Each time Daddy worked on that vehicle, more smoke came from Mommy's nose and ears than actually came from the motor of our car. Mommy's only love for that car was when it was functional.

Often when Mommy drove, Winky and I fought for whose turn it was to sit in the front seat. As much as we fought we still couldn't stay away from each other. On one occasion while Mommy was driving the car, Winky and I had a dispute. All of a sudden the car began to slow down and then it stopped dead in its tracks. At first I thought Winky and I were in trouble, but then I realized we all might be in trouble. The motor of our car had cut off and we were right in the middle of the railroad tracks. From a distance we could see the train and hear its whistle.

Mommy tried to start the car, but all the motor did was cough and putt. The railroad signals began to flash. The crossing bell went Ding! Ding! Ding! The railroad crossing gates stretched from one side of the street to the other. There was one crossing gate behind us and another in front.

Panic had now found its way to Mommy's powdered face. Her nose began to perspire and the water from her eyes made its own set of railroad tracks. With one hand, Mommy held tightly to the steering wheel, and with her other hand she down-shifted the gear stick attached to the steering collar. With one foot she patted the gas pedal, and with the other foot she popped the clutch.

All that shifting, patting, and popping did not do a bit of good. Mommy said, "Oh my goodness!" and then she called on the Lord for mercy, but that did not start the car. To hear her call on the Lord in church was one thing, but to hear her call on the Lord in a crisis was another.

Between the sound of the oncoming train and the look on Mommy's face, it felt as if our world was about to come to an end.

As the train got closer, Mommy shouted to us, "GET OUT OF THE CAR!"

Winky had climbed over the front seat before I could open the passenger door. He was right on my heels as I got out of the car. This was one time that Mommy did not have to speak to us twice.

We got out on the passenger side and ran around the front of the car to the driver's side. Mommy stood in back of the car out of harm's way. My brother and I clung tightly to her coat.

The train whistle must have made Mommy very nervous. Each time it blew, she screamed.

Our car had just died on the railroad tracks and now it looked as if it was going to get killed. I was a little surprised to see how frantic Mommy had become. As much as she hated that car, I thought that this would be the perfect opportunity for it to get replaced.

The train was getting closer. Fortunately it was also slowing down, but that did not stop the engineer from blowing the train whistle.

After coming within a few inches of hitting our car, the train came to a complete halt.

The engineer was laughing as Mommy's tears turned into joy.

On each side of the railroad tracks a line of several automobiles waited behind the safety of the crossing gates. From the line of cars in back of us came two white men dressed in white-collared shirts and suit jackets. As they approached our car, Winky and I continued to hold dearly onto Mommy's coat. One of the white men walked around to the front of the car and asked if we needed any assistance. The other white man asked Mommy whether the carburetor was flooded because he smelled gas. The one that asked if we needed assistance wanted to see if he could start the engine of our car. Mommy didn't seem to mind because she stretched her arm out and gave him the key.

After putting the car in gear and holding the clutch pedal to the floor, he turned the ignition key. His eyes went straight to the dashboard meters and then he turned off the key. He nodded his head as if he had figured out the problem. As he got out of the car he looked at Mommy and asked, "Miss, did you run out of gas?"

Mommy tried to look surprised, but the look on her face was more of embarrassment. In order to get the show back on the road, the men that had offered to help Mommy start our car also offered to push it off the tracks and safely to the side of the road.

In that frightening experience, I learned that when I grew up and had my own car, I would never make the mistake of running out of gas.

RAILROAD CROSSING #2

It was hurricane season. The rain came down like cats and dogs. Winky and I got soaked from head to toe as we walked home from school. After crossing the last set of railroad tracks, a white lady in an automobile stopped her car and asked us if we wanted a ride. Winky looked tempted and I said no, but the lady insisted anyway. As wet as we were we couldn't get any wetter so I pulled my brother away from the curb and told him to come on.

Mommy had specifically warned us to never talk to strangers. For what it was worth, being alive and wet was better than to be found in some other unfortunate circumstance.

On another occasion, I was late for school. Winky was sick and stayed home. All the other children had walked on to school and I had to walk by myself.

Shortly after I left the house, I heard the whistle of the train. The road leading to the railroad tracks came to a deep bend. Although I couldn't see the train, I clearly heard its whistle.

As I got closer to the tracks, I could see that it was too late. The freight workers were unhitching cargo to be dropped off and hitching another set of cargo to leave.

While waiting, I was approached by a smiling colored man dressed in denim overalls. While my ears were filled with the sounds from the railroad alarms, another alarm also rang loudly, sending warning signs inside my head. Although he was a colored railroad man, he was also a stranger! He reminded me of the Big Bad Wolf in "Little Red Riding Hood." As he drew closer, my body nearly shook because I was nervous that he might try to touch me.

"Hey, little girl, you sure are cute. Don't you know that you are a cute little girl?"

What was he expecting me to say? What was his point? It didn't matter if I was ugly or cute, all I knew was this colored man was a stranger, and instead of talking to me, he should have been attending to his railroad business.

The railroad signals made it difficult for me to hear the other things the "stranger" said. I felt uncomfortable. Lucky for me, the trains started moving again. When the tracks were cleared, I ran straight to the corner of Hickory and Maple. I was so glad to see Miss Addie. She was the crossing guard. I wanted to tell her about the stranger, the colored man, the railroad man who had just talked to me and told me that I was cute. But she was already hollering and seemed awfully annoyed.

"Come on, slow poke!"

After I crossed the street, I looked back at her and all she did was yell at me and insist that I run to school. So I ran to school as if I was running for my life. The school yard was empty; the late bell had just rung. It felt as if my heart was going to beat right out of my chest. I was exhausted from running and dreadfully afraid of the colored railroad man who was also a stranger.

Miss Bliss was not happy about me being tardy. Even though I ran to get to my classroom, she did not excuse me for being late. During the school day that stranger's face flashed several times across my mind. There was no sense in telling Miss Bliss. She wouldn't have believed me anyway. She never cared for me before so why would she care for me now?

After detention, I walked home by myself. Before I got to the corner of Maple and Hickory, I heard the railroad crossing bells. DING! DING! DING! Each *ding* made my heart go *dong*. I did not want to be late getting home and I didn't want to see that stranger again. I ran all the way to the railroad tracks hoping that I could make it to the other side.

By the time I got to the railroad tracks, it was too late. My heart almost stopped when I saw the trains slowing down. I could not believe it was happening all over again. There he was dressed in his overalls, the same railroad man, the same stranger, the same colored man standing alongside the tracks as if he had been waiting for me all day. Again he approached me. I did not trust his smile. His fangs were covered in gold. He may have been a railroad man, but he was a stranger, and all that gold he had on his teeth also made him look like a pirate.

None of my friends were around. It was just me and him. I began to walk to the other side of the road, but he stepped right in front of me and knelt close to the ground and repeated what he had said to me that morning.

"Hey, little girl, you sure are cute." And then he said, "My wife and children haven't kissed me today, can you just give me a kiss?"

As he pointed to the side of his face where he wanted me to kiss him, I shook my head from left to right, indicating that I did not want to kiss him. Slowly I backed away from him. While backing away I wanted to shout, "Leave me alone! I am not Little Red Riding Hood!"

One of the railroad engineers spoke to him and urged him to come along so that they could finish their work.

Of course Mommy was very upset because I arrived home late. I told her about the stranger, the railroad man who was also colored and had gold teeth. She reported him to the police and I never saw him again. I learned from that experience that Mommy was right: walking alone can be dangerous and safety does come in numbers.

IN THE PINK

When my parents had a discussion about getting a car, I thought they were talking about getting a new car. The thought of getting a new car was exciting. As it turned out, it was only a thought—my thought.

When I found out it was a used car, I was a little disappointed, but whatever it was, it had to be better than what we already had.

It was a 1953 pink Nash Ambassador. I felt proud having a car the same color as our house. I've said before that pride comes before the fall. The kids in my neighborhood already thought the color of our house was odd, but when they found out that we now had a pink car that matched our house they just laughed themselves pink. I learned to ignore those perpetrators. At least we had a car that rolled and its front seat went back like a recliner.

I knew living in a pink house and having a pink car was not an everyday normal thing, but it was much more than what we used to have. There were times when some of their laughter went too far. To be the nice person that Daddy wanted me to be, I acted as if their mockery did not hurt me.

Daddy also admitted that he was teased about the car. He said one of his coworkers had a slogan for him: "When you buy a Nash, you buy the best. You drive ten miles and walk the rest."

That was one true slogan. Daddy didn't have to wait too long before he found out what it meant.

One afternoon while he was working on the motor, the car went out of gear. It rolled backwards. The door to the back seat on the passenger's side was opened. The door got hung up on one of the trees that stood alongside our driveway. The door was practically torn off, but at least it stopped the car from going out into the street.

Daddy had to replace the car door. No matter what he did, he could not get the door to shut properly. In order to keep the door closed, it had to be locked.

One afternoon Daddy took the family for a ride. Mommy wanted to stop at Sears department store to pay on a few items she had laid away. When we reached our destination, I automatically opened the back door on the passenger's side. Mommy told me to stay in the car and sit with Winky because he was asleep. When I reached over to wake him, Mommy told me to close the door and stay in the car.

On the way home riding on Motleys Lane, my door on the passenger's side swung open. I was leaning on the door when it happened. It was the door that Daddy had replaced. The window of the door was rolled down. Most likely it was my weight that caused the door to open. I held on to the door as long as I could. I was in shock. I couldn't scream; I hung on for my dear life. The next curve in the road threw me away from the door.

I fell to the asphalt and rolled to the rocky side of the road. The last thing I remember seeing of that car was its back tire as it rolled away. I continued to roll like a hotdog out of its bun. At the time I was not aware that I had rolled past a guard rail.

I continued to roll down an embankment full of bushes, weeds, and tall trees.

When the rolling stopped, I landed less than three feet away from a river. I did not know where I was. All I could see was rocky soil and tall grass. After looking up to the blue sky I did not waste another minute. I stood as fast as I could. The first thing I did was look at my hands and knees. Blood was everywhere! I was horrified and I began to feel pain all over my body.

After taking in what I saw of my wounds, I began to look around in hopes of seeing my parents, but they were not there. Having no sight of them brought me even more pain. The abrasions that were not covered in mud exposed the blood that dripped from the tender white meat of my flesh. Although I was petrified and in pain, I could not just allow myself to stand there. I tried to run, but I couldn't lift my foot. One of my shoes went down in the mud. With my bleeding hands I grabbed onto the nearest bush and pulled my foot out to a more secure part of the ground. It wasn't easy, but I had to practically crawl away from the river bank and back to the road.

All I thought about was getting back to my parents. I hoped with all my heart that they would come back for me. As I got closer to the guard rail, I could hear the sound of cars passing by.

After getting past the guard rail and onto the gravel, I took another look at my elbows, hands, and knees. None of my limbs looked like they belonged to me. The pain was unbelievable. What was even more unbelievable was that I didn't see our pink car.

When the car finally came into view, it looked as if it was a mile away. Daddy was driving the car in reverse. I ran as fast as my legs could take me. I was so glad to see that car, I was so happy they found me. When Daddy stopped the car, Mommy got out and looked at me. I was in hysterics. She closed the back door of the car and told me to sit between her and Daddy.

All the way to the hospital, Daddy drove like he was driving an ambulance. He carried me into the emergency room. Crying loudly got me all the attention I needed. The doctors and nurses treated me right away.

The necessary measure of care was much less than I expected. My arms and legs weren't broken, but it sure felt like it. I expected a plaster cast along with a wheelchair and a set of crutches.

I was completely bandaged from arm to arm and leg to leg, but of course that would not garner the same attention as a plaster cast. I wanted to be autographed. After being accidently thrown out of the car and receiving multiple wounds, I thought I deserved a wheelchair. I was so sure no one would expect me walk under those conditions. With Daddy by my side I bravely asked, "Daddy, can I have a wheelchair?"

"Why do you need a wheelchair?"

"My legs hurt. I can't walk! Please, can I have a wheelchair, Daddy?"

"You are going to be sore, but you can walk. You do not need a wheelchair."

"Well, can I have crutches?"

"I don't think you need crutches."

There was no one to plead my case. The doctors and nurses just looked at me. They seemed to be saying something in their own unspoken language. Mommy also agreed with Daddy.

No one seemed to understand how I felt. My wounds were real. My bandages were obvious. Each pain had a scream of its own. No matter how I moved, each throb was painful.

After all, my bandages were justifiable. To be given a wheelchair or a set of crutches would have made the hurt rewardingly better. For years Winky was the one who got all the attention: nose bleeds, hospitalizations, and every week he was taken to the clinic for injections to treat his bronchitis. Any type of apparatus for me would have served me as a golden prize.

They must have known that I was being melodramatic. Perhaps I was asking for too much. After all, when the accident occurred, I was able to get up and climb back to the road and run to the car.

The whole outcome could have been worse. I should have been more grateful. Daddy helped me to keep my dignity by picking me up in his arms and carrying me out of the emergency room and back to the car.

For about a week my body really ached. I continued to sulk over the fact that I had no medical apparatuses to assist me. After a couple weeks of recuperation, Daddy came home with the best apparatus ever.

From my bedroom window I could see him riding up and down the street on a girl's bicycle. I had to refrain myself from jumping out of my bed. Instead of going outside I hollered from my bedroom window, "Daddy, whose bicycle are you riding?"

He gave me the best answer I ever heard: "Yours, when you get better."

Although the bicycle was purchased from a junk yard, I didn't mind. It was better than anything the doctor could have ordered.

The bicycle had seen better days. The paint was weather-beaten. The front tire was bigger than the back. Its rims were rusty, and it came with no fenders. Regardless of all the flaws, I did not complain. I was so grateful that this treasure belonged to me.

Just knowing that I would soon be taught to ride the bicycle was therapeutic enough for me. There was no wheelchair in the world more appealing than the wheels on a bicycle. Having a bicycle lifted my spirits and made me feel more "in the pink."

My lesson from that experience was to always make sure that the car doors are properly closed and locked after getting into a car.

BALLERINA

During my recuperation, Cherry and I spent a lot of time under the big oak tree in her front yard. Her mother didn't allow her to play in the sun because she didn't want Cherry to get too dark. We played board games, we played with our dolls, and we talked. Cherry did most of the talking. I learned a lot that summer just by listening to her speak. It was amusing to hear her mystic stories about the treasures that could be found only in the attic of her house.

Almost every day she talked about her beautiful pink ballerina slippers. She explained that the slippers could make her dance and twirl like a real ballerina. When I asked to see her ballerina slippers, she said the slippers were in the attic. She also said if the slippers were removed from the attic, they would no longer have their magic.

There was another story she told about an old boot that left a dime each day underneath its sole. Again her disclaimer was that it only worked in her attic. I really wanted to see her collection of dolls from all over the world, but she said that her father had packed them away in a wooden box until she got a little older. I began to suspect that her collected treasures were only hidden in the attic of her imagination.

My cousin P.J. was just the opposite. She did not brag about her toys. Any toy she spoke about having was tangible.

P.J. had more than enough toys in her toy boxes to open up her own toy store. Not only did P.J. have all of the dolls advertised on television, but she also had all the top ten board games and many other toys that were made for all children.

P.J. was so much fun to be around; she was very generous. Not only did she let me play with her toys, she also always sent me home with something to keep. Cherry may have had all the imaginary treasures, but P.J. had the real goods.

P.J.'s mom, Aunt Essie, was always generous in giving me P.J.'s outgrown dresses and shoes. Her Sunday dresses were always beautiful and when wearing them I always felt like the ballerina. I always felt like the luckiest person in the world when I wore her Buster Brown shoes.

Each week I looked forward to seeing P.J. at church and at school. Although she only lived across town, my biggest wish was for her to become one of my next door neighbors. Each time we came together we jumped up and down as if we had not seen each other for a long time.

CHAPTER 16

MRS. BOOKMAN

The only favorable thing that Miss Bliss did for me was to promote me to the fourth grade. I was so happy about going to the next grade that I did not care who was going to be my next teacher as long as it wasn't Miss Bliss.

People at church and people at school thought P.J. and I were sisters. We were the same age, but she was one grade ahead of me because she started kindergarten one year before me. Not only did she pass to the fifth grade, but that June of 1961 she also graduated to Fillmore Jr. High School. Lots of excitement rang out amongst her and all the other graduating students of her class. I wanted to be happy for her, but I felt left out. Cambridge Elementary School was only a block away from Fillmore Jr. High School, and Spano's Candy Store was in between. In the future I would meet her at the candy store after school.

That summer Mulberry had a sudden increase in population and I had to be transferred to Fillmore Jr. High. For me that was a miracle! A few of my classmates felt a little cheated because we did not get to have a graduating ceremony for leaving Cambridge Elementary School. On the other hand, I felt I had won a grand prize.

Fillmore Jr. High was a very big school with many classrooms. It now ranged from the fourth grade to the eighth grade. Although it was a very large school, it was not big enough to keep me from finding my cousin P.J. Being transferred now made it possible for me to see her every day at lunch and after school.

I had the feeling that it was going to be a very good school year. Cherry was also transferred, but she was in room fourteen and I was in room fifteen. This was the first time Cherry and I had different classrooms since first grade.

My teacher was Avery Bookman. She was the first colored teacher hired in the town of Mulberry. I felt lucky, proud, and honored to have her as my teacher. I promised myself that I would work very hard to get decent grades so that she could be proud of me too.

There were thirty students in Mrs. Bookman's class and the ratio was one colored student to every five white students. It felt so good to have that amount of colored children in my classroom.

I continued to hide the hairline of my forehead by keeping the front part of my hair curled into bangs. I thought if I kept my forehead covered no one could judge the level of my IQ. At that time I still believed that all people with higher foreheads were smarter than people with lower foreheads.

Mrs. Bookman showed our class how to use the school library. Index cards were filed in long rectangular wooden drawers that slid inside of a wooden cabinet. I was amazed to learn that our library filing system was the same as libraries all over the world.

I was careful when choosing my books because I was a very slow reader. The books I took out were filled with illustrations that told me enough of what I needed to know about the story. Sometimes I spent more time looking at the pictures than reading the book. Trying to sound out all those words was too distracting. Truthfully speaking, most of my books were never read.

I didn't mind learning songs. I loved singing what we sang in church and also what we sang in school. I had no problems learning the words. The songs on the radio were also easy to learn. I remembered every fairy tale story that was told to me. Commercial jingles were also easy to learn, but when it came to reading and comprehension, that was a different story. Math was almost impossible to do without using my little fingers.

My mind was resistant to school books. I wanted so badly to learn from Mrs. Bookman, but the crickets in my head were just too loud. Studying was excruciating because it took me away from La-La Land.

Our class performed in a play called *Alice in Wonderland*. Everyone in my classroom had a part in the play. This was the first class play in which I performed. I was dressed like a bunny rabbit. My lines were mute and I hopped around on stage. I hoped that this was not going to be a sign. Who wants to be a dumb bunny all their life?

I don't believe Mrs. Bookman had any teacher's pets. She did not allow any ethnic or religious groups to be first on the food chain. If there were any such favorites, she kept it to herself.

Unfortunately, the next set of fourth graders did not have the privilege of being taught by Mrs. Bookman. She found employment in another township. Later I learned that she was fed up with the crude hostility of Mulberry's board of education.

In the year 1965, Mrs. Bookman's husband made history. He was a part of the board of education in another county. Serving as plaintiff, he opened a case in the New Jersey Supreme Court, Bookman vs. Board of Education. Mr. Bookman won his case in putting an end to "neighborhood districting" in New Jersey's public schools.

When I attended Stony Brook Elementary, I was one of the victims of their racial segregation in the neighborhood districting. I went from being in a school that was all colored to being in a school that was predominantly white. That is why I thought I was in *Rumpus Room*.

I will always consider Mrs. Bookman to be one of the bravest patriots. She was the first Negro teacher in Mulberry. Although she did not stay, she broke ground for other Afro American teachers who taught in Mulberry.

CARTMAN VERSUS GORDEN

Cherry Gorden had a way of catching me off guard because she tricked me with her words. For example, she would say something negative about herself and get me to go along with her and then she would celebrate her success by kicking me.

She treated me like a donkey and she kicked like a mule. She was always unpredictable. When she thought she was cute, she would talk in her sweet ballerina voice. When she studied her lesson for test day, her words flew from her mouth like a rocket. On the days she did not talk to me, she either ignored me or kicked me.

I told Mommy how Cherry could be nice one minute and mean the next. Mommy spoke with Cherry's mother, but their conversation ended in angry words. After that Mommy gave me permission to defend myself. Daddy suggested that I shouldn't fight because Mrs. Gorden was very ill. Daddy had more sympathy for Cherry's mother than he had for me. Cherry's mother and Daddy used to walk to school and play together when they were children. When Daddy was building our house she made him iced tea and lemonade during the summer and hot tea and coffee in the winter. But what did all that tea have to do with me? I tried to understand his point, but all I felt were the points of Cherry's shoes.

When I told my cousin P.J. what Cherry had done to me...
ha! She was furious! P.J. caught Cherry in the girls' room and
gave her a good lesson on who not to kick. Cherry must have
been scared for her life because she reported P.J. to the principal's office. P.J. was almost suspended. I believe it was my
cousin's prestige that kept her afloat. P.J. was an "A" student
and on the student council. She was a good team player in girls'
basketball. Besides, she was well liked by many teachers and
many students both colored and white. Cherry also was an "A"
student, but she did not have the prestige.

When all the colored students of Fillmore Jr. High School
heard that Cherry had reported P.J., a snowball of anger rolled
from one person to the next. Everyone wanted to get Cherry.
When Cherry found out how desperately everyone wanted to
fight her, she went crying to her teacher. For the next three
weeks Cherry had her own personal chauffeur. Her teacher's
station wagon was what saved her.

It was on one of Cherry's friendly days when she finally
shared with me that her mother had cancer. She explained to
me that her father was the cause because he beat her mother
in the chest. I felt bad for Cherry, but not enough to make it
okay for her to keep kicking me. Too bad Cherry's ballerina
shoes weren't real because my cousin really kept Cherry on
her toes.

SOCIAL PROMOTION

Okay! What was the big deal? So what if I did not pass the
fourth grade with flying colors? Some call it social promotion;
others call it slowpoke promotion. One thing for sure, it might
have been by the skin of my teeth, but at least I was in motion.

Yes, I had to go to summer school, but wasn't that a small price to pay? At least I did not have to repeat the fourth grade. I know it was a miracle and I felt lucky.

Five is the number for grace. In the Bible it says that David the shepherd boy picked five smooth stones to war against Goliath. I'm not bragging, but I know it was Mrs. Bookman's grace that promoted me to the fifth grade.

The moment I set foot in my fifth-grade class I felt I was in the Promised Land. Once again I felt privileged to have an Afro American teacher. Her name was Mrs. Morris. She looked so much like the wife of our civil rights leader. Sometimes I suspected that she was his wife and she was here to investigate the way that Mulberry's board of education treated Mrs. Bookman.

Mrs. Morris probably called me sleeping beauty. At school, sleeping was easy. At least the *Witch* did not bother me in class. After getting home from school, I took a nap. At night I was afraid to go to sleep because the *Witch* had a bad habit of visiting me during the night. Many nights I would stay awake so that the *Witch* would not bother me. Sometimes I wished I had someone to talk to about it.

I hated the *Witch*! What gave it the right to come in my bedroom at night? Why did it attack me while I was asleep? What did it want from me? What could I do to make it stop? It would not have been so bad if I could have screamed or made some sound so that Winky could have heard me. Why me? I often wondered why the *Witch* never bothered him.

Shortly before Thanksgiving of 1962 I received the best news ever. My Uncle Jack bought a house right on Hickory Street. My cousin P.J. and I were soon to be neighbors. We could wave at each other from the front of our homes. After crossing the beginning of my street I could step on the sidewalk and into her yard. As for me, this was more than just a miracle, it was a dream come true. Every day we saw each other. Either

I went to her house or she came to mine. Every time I saw my cousin it felt like Christmas.

Two other families moved to our neighborhood. Both families had ten-year-old daughters, the same age as P.J. and me. One of the girls was Gracie Williams and the other girl was named Terry Cooper. Both girls had fairer skin and longer hair, but that didn't keep them from playing with P.J. and me. Gracie was in the same grade as P.J. and Terry was in the same grade as me. Although the four of us were more like a clique, I felt I was the luckiest one of them all because P.J. was more than just my cousin; she was my four-leaf clover. Cherry tried her best to blend in with our clique. We did not mind talking to her, but when she wasn't around we really talked about her.

The only thing missing from our clique was brand-new bicycles. That November of 1962, we all made a pact. We vowed to do whatever it took to get a new bike for Christmas and there was no shame to my game. I did not care if I had to get down on my knees and beg. I told my parents exactly what kind of bicycle I wanted. I dreamed about that bike! Even when I was awake I saw myself riding it.

Surely with all the money Daddy made working overtime, he had saved enough to pay "Santa Claus." Yes! I said "Santa Claus." I wasn't a fool. Clayton tried to tell me that "Santa" did not exist. Mommy on the other hand reminded me that not believing meant "Santa" did not have to bring any presents.

That Christmas Eve I thought about hiding all our pepper shakers from Santa. I wanted to see him for myself. What more did I have to lose? The only thing I wanted to see from "Santa" was my brand-new bike. I didn't want to be the only one amongst my friends without one.

That junkyard bike did not cut it anymore. Please don't misunderstand me. I wasn't trying to be ungrateful. My brother and I rode the bike almost every day. I believe we fixed the flats more than we actually rode the bike. Even if we had painted it, the bike still would have looked ugly. Whether I got a brand-new bike or not, that bike was history!

On Christmas Eve I slept with my fingers crossed and my toes crossed. My brother wanted a brand-new bicycle too, but I was the first to ask for one. I also wanted a doll, but not as bad as I wanted a brand-new bike. As it turned out, Santa honored my request. Winky also got a brand-new bike.

My bicycle was blue. It was the most beautiful bike I had ever laid my eyes on. Everything about it shone. The handle bar was all chrome. Blue and white streamers hung from each handle grip. The neck of the bike had battery-operated lights. Both wheels were chrome. The rubber on the tires smelled heavenly. Each tire had fenders. A blue rack sat over its back fender.

I wanted so bad to thank Santa, but unfortunately I fell asleep before his arrival. Having that bike made me so happy. "Santa" also gave me a doll. I promised myself that I would thank him next Christmas—that was, of course, if there really was a "Santa."

Indeed I did thank my parents with lots of hugs and kisses. I knew it was really because of them that I had the merriest Christmas ever. This was also one of the merriest Christmases for my other three friends. "Santa" had enough bikes for them too.

Mrs. Morris was an excellent teacher and I know I would have been one of her excellent students if I had stayed awake in her class. It's a wonder I learned anything that year. Some may say that it was social promotion and others may say it was a miracle, but I say it was grace. As I said before, five is the number for grace. Being that I had Mrs. Morris as my fifth-grade teacher, I wished I also had her for sixth.

In the summer of '63 Daddy took us on vacation. We took a trip to North Carolina. I thought we would never get there. Every time we went over one mountain there was always another one to follow. We visited Daddy's parents and stayed with them too. I always looked forward to seeing my grandparents. I loved visiting their house and I felt so much love in their home. Not only was this the place of my father's family history, but there was also something familiar there too. I had never lived there, but it felt as if I had. Granddaddy was always laughing and joking. He raised hound dogs. He was also a good hunter and fisherman. Grandma was full of hugs, her food was always good, and I couldn't get enough of their refreshing well water. There were other relatives and childhood friends that Daddy wanted to visit, but when they heard we were in town they came by to visit us.

My parents were always talking with the other grown-ups about old times. They often talked about different superstitions. Some tales were silly. I didn't mind listening as long as they weren't talking about ghosts. Granddaddy loved to laugh and loved to talk about ghosts. He seemed to be very brave, but from what I heard, the sight of a bull frog could make him run out of town.

Winky and I shared the convertible sofa in my grandparents' living room. At night the room was pitch black. Every night I woke up and heard footsteps walking across that room. I couldn't see anyone and I was too afraid to ask for their name. The thing that bothered me the most was that every time I fell asleep I'd wake up to a set of footsteps sliding across the floor. Because of the dark, I was not able to see. I tried not to panic, but whoever or whatever was inside that room also seemed to be keeping me from being able to move or speak. At the time I felt the *Witch* had followed me from New Jersey, or perhaps it was one of the ghosts that Granddaddy often spoke about. Either way, I was spooked because I felt it came from the supernatural.

While riding back to New Jersey, I questioned Daddy about the strange footsteps I heard and the feeling of people moving about that room during the night. When he confirmed that it may have been spirits I heard, the fuzzy hairs stood on the back of my neck and also the goose bumps on my arms.

Daddy went on to say that when he was a small boy his cousin choked on a boiled egg and died in that house. For one week his cousin's body was laid out to view in the very room I was sleeping in.

For the remainder of the trip I did not engage in any more gobbledygook stories about spirits. I already had the *Witch* tagging along with me and did not want any more of its "company" haunting along to get me. As far as I was concerned, what happened in North Carolina could stay in North Carolina.

CHAPTER 17

LEFT BEHIND

The Bible says that on the sixth day God created man. Giants like Goliath had six fingers and six toes. Six was also the number of our house on "purgatory" Pine Street. Although I was six years old when we happily moved to Mulberry, I don't feel that six was ever my lucky number. There were six more weeks of school and during that time strange things were happening to me while I was asleep. Almost every night I had a reoccurring dream about me being chased by a set of hands. All around me was darkness except for a searchlight that also came from behind me like a shadow. From that light I could only see a set of hands that appeared to be slightly darker than the light. No matter how fast I ran, I was always within inches of being caught. When I could no longer run from exhaustion, I would fall to the ground and collapse. When I was touched by those chasing hands, I would instantly wake up feeling as if the dream really did happen. Perhaps I was developing some kind of sixth sense, but what did I know?

Being exhausted like that always left me open for the *Witch*. Why was all this happening? What was the purpose of going to sleep if I couldn't get any rest? When I was asleep I went from being chased by a set of grayish hands to being ridden by the *Witch*. Also, I began to feel that I was having out-of-body experiences. Often I thought I was walking through the house and then at some point I'd wake up to find myself still in the bed. As puzzling as it was, at least I was able to move, but if I didn't get out of the bed right away, it would simply happen again.

P.J. said being in the sixth grade was easy. I knew she was right, but was there anything too hard for P.J.? Our last names were the same, but like a set of batteries, she was the positive and I was the negative. When P.J. did her chores, zip! zip! zip! She was done. When I did my chores, tick-tock, tick-tock, tick-tock, time just stood still. P.J. could whistle through her school homework. Each time I did mine it was like taking a crash course. In gymnastics P.J. was very good at doing somersaults, back flips, and jumping hurdles. As for me, I was lucky if I could do a forward roll.

P.J.'s energy was always productive, as opposed to Emily Trout's energy. After all the battles I had with the *Witch* I was lucky to have any energy at all. Biologically, all our bodies were taking shape. Around my peers I had no problem showing off my upper body form. But when I was around grown-ups or my dad, I hunched my shoulders forward so that my chest would look flat like pancakes.

Grown-ups often forgot how embarrassing it was when they traveled the road of puberty. In most cases it was my older relatives that looked at me as if to say, "O-o-o, look at you, you are becoming a young lady."

From the moment I stepped into my sixth-grade classroom, any luck I ever had must have blown right out of that classroom window. I could not believe my teacher was a man. How did he ever get to be a sixth-grade teacher? Whoever heard of a man teaching in a one-class setting with children all day? He must have gotten his ride on the band wagon of civil rights.

Yuk! He still gives me the creeps! His name was Mr. Kleinberg. The top of his hair was almost bald. In his attempts to cover it he combed one side of his hair over to the other side of his head. On Fridays and certain religious holidays he wore a yarmulke. Wearing that little cap did not fool me. He may have looked religious but was he righteous?

He had several bad habits such as moving his knees in and out when he sat at his desk, digging in his ears, and jingling his pocket change.

Mr. Kleinberg also had a few nuts and bolts that jingled in his head. He grinned like a fox. His teeth wouldn't have looked so bad if it weren't for the tobacco stains. He also dressed in sheep's clothing. He had a big flaky forehead, and his hair also had flakes. As a matter of fact, everything about him was flakey.

His desk was in front of the class. If any of the girls sat with their legs wider than the gap of his front teeth, he would automatically squint his eyes. His squint made it sometimes difficult for me to see which girl was the victim of his lustful eyes. Sometime it seemed as if he was trying to make his sight pierce through the threads of his victim's underwear. If Mommy had invisible eyes then surely he had X-ray eyes.

Our seats were connected to our desks, which made it impossible to reposition our seats. My desk was the last desk in the front row. Often when Mr. Kleinberg walked around the classroom to observe our work, it was always the papers on my desk that whistled and betrayed me. Even if Clayton was in my classroom, he wouldn't have been too much help.

His method of teaching me made my teeth cringe. I didn't mind him touching my papers but it never ended there. He was sly like a fox. One of his hands would be on my papers and the other rubbing my back. If this is what it meant being the teacher's pet then I didn't want it. When he got bored doing that, he would inconspicuously take the hand that was on my papers and move them to the front of my blouse. To avoid that I kept the front of my chest guarded so that he wouldn't rub me the wrong way. How could anything be learned under those circumstances? It was bad enough that math was always trick-bla-ometry, but now his tricky moves made my math lessons more like trick-pornography.

Sure, I could have reported him, but what good would that have done? Of course he would have retaliated by discrediting my grades. Who would have believed me anyway? I was colored and he was white.

In that year of 1963 our class performed in a school play called *The Christmas Carol*. I felt very left out because my grades did not make the cut to perform in the school play. I believe his decision to leave me out of the play was really based upon how much he achieved in his "hands-on tutoring." But as a consolation prize he let me help prepare the props and fill in as an understudy for the play. Wow! What a joke. What poor student was likely to miss out on their big debut?

At that time things seemed to change quickly in America. It was just a little over a year ago that we'd shot our first space ship into orbit. That was one of our biggest accomplishments. Our biggest loss that year was when our thirty-fifth president was shot. His assassination was a Thanksgiving nightmare. People all over the world were shocked. It felt as if the whole earth came to a complete stop.

Rex Briggs was one of my classmates. We exchanged phone numbers and he would not stop calling me. He was handsome. Half the girls at church and school wanted him, but that did not impress me. I decided to keep it simple and just stay friends. To have him as a boyfriend and then break up with me would have been too heartbreaking and too embarrassing. Being in Mr. Kleinberg's class was already hard, why make it harder?

When the month of June came, I was about the happiest person in the world. I was already singing, "No more teachers, no more books, no more Mr. Kleinberg's perverted looks." I was on my way out of the sixth grade and into the seventh.

That last parent/teacher conference with Mr. Kleinberg was one experience I will never forget. Midway through the conference Mr. Kleinberg nervously moved his legs in and out and up and down. What he reported to my mother took a turn for the worst. If my report card was a music sheet, it would have been written in D flat and F sharp.

Of course he'd never give me credit for keeping his "sleight of the hands" movements from the front of my blouse and to my "B" cup. He said, "I have no choice but to repeat her. I offered her my help, but she never came to me after school for help."

I almost got sick when he looked at me and asked, "Why didn't you come to me after school for help?"

All year long he had stripped me with his lustful eyes. I wanted to strip him down to who he really was, but instead I pleaded to be sent to summer school. He shook his head and said no. That was one of the worst days of my life!

He made himself look like the good professor. I felt hurt and humiliated and I was angry! How was I ever going to be able to face anyone about this matter? I could not even face myself.

Too bad Mommy didn't know the truth. If I had told her about him touching me, would she have believed me? If Daddy had found out, he probably would have gone to jail for killing Mr. Kleinberg. I know our civil rights leader would have wanted to help, but with all the freedom marches going on, he had bigger fish to fry.

At that point, who would have believed me? Mulberry was Mulberry, and at that time, white was always right.

Just as I had suspected from day one, the moment I entered that class, all my luck blew right out of the window. The summer of 1964 I walked in a wilderness of gloom and doom. A cloud of shame hung over my head by day and then it would burst into a river of hot tears at night. My parents did not have to worry about punishing me. For forty-eight dreadful summer days and forty-eight dreadful summer nights I grounded myself.

Everyone else had passed on to the next grade. How could I celebrate with them? I was hurt and I felt stupid. I didn't want to face anyone. I contemplated faking a nervous breakdown. Acting catatonic sounded like the easiest way to go. All I had to do was lie in bed and stare at the ceiling.

I decided not to go that route because the smell of bacon would blow my cover. If P.J. came over and tickled me, that would also give me away. If I faked it too well, a straightjacket would have been my only Emmy. I wanted to hide, but not in a mental hospital.

After forty-eight dreadful summer days and forty-eight dreadful nights, I finally came to my senses. Clayton helped me to realize that there was more to life than just crying every night. He said that all my tears would not change my situation. He said the only person who could change my situation was me. My grades did look like a drums music sheet. Promoting me probably wouldn't have helped me, but that didn't mean that Mr. Kleinberg did me a favor.

Daddy always said I could learn anything I wanted. I believed him, but I also needed help. For the rest of the summer I went to bed early so that I could spend more time on my knees to ask God to open up my mind and make me smart like everyone else.

While I wasted most of the summer feeling sorry for myself, Cherry Gorden was hurting too. My parents visited Cherry's mother in the hospital. Mommy said she couldn't believe her eyes. Mrs. Gorden was down to skin and bones. She also said that Mrs. Gorden apologized for feuding over Cherry. Mommy assured Mrs. Gorden that she was forgiven. Mrs. Gorden died two days after that visit. As for Cherry, what pain could be worse than that? I will never forget the look on her face at her mother's burial. Cherry's eyes stayed fixed upon her mother's coffin. Her eyebrows looked almost like caterpillars as they moved upon her brow. Her lips stayed pressed together as they moved from one side of her face to the other.

Cherry looked like she wanted to be right with her mother. All I saw in her face was pain and emptiness. Regardless of all the people that came to give their last respects, she reached out to no one. It would not have surprised me if she had gotten out of her seat and jumped into that grave.

Two days after her mother's funeral, Cherry began to demonstrate bizarre behavior. She could not cope with the loss of her mother. I am not sure what kind of cocoon she had spun herself into, but it landed her in a diagnostic hospital for children.

Cherry's grief was far more than mine. My repeating the sixth grade did not compare with how she was left behind. Her nervous breakdown was understandable. The death of Mrs. Gorden taught me to be grateful for what I had. Getting left behind in the sixth grade was definitely a great disappointment, but it certainly was not the end of the world.

MRS. MOLNAR

Just to think about school shopping normally made me want to jump, skip, and whistle, but like a torch, I passed all that enthusiasm on to Mommy.

Most of my school shopping took place at Learners department store. All of the latest fashions for teenage girls could be found there.

Mini dresses and miniskirts were on the rise, but Mommy wasn't ready for me to wear them. Every dress and skirt she bought me came right to my knees. Mommy was adamant about me wearing long-line girdles. Although they made me look firm on the outside, I felt shaky on the inside. Those girdles gave me paranoid tendencies. When people smiled at me, I wondered, were they smiling at me or at my girdle?

Repeating the sixth grade did not mean I knew exactly what to expect. Inside my head there were still a lot of "what ifs." I heard that my new teacher was strict and mean. What did it matter anyway? I had nothing else to lose. She couldn't be any worse than Miss Bliss.

I felt like the dunce of the school. Getting through the first day would be a great miracle within itself. The only thing I needed was courage. I could barely face myself let alone others.

On that first day of school I had planned to act invisible. I did not want to talk to anyone. I was not going to let anyone get me in trouble. For reassurance, I held on to my pretentious pout.

My new teacher's name was Mrs. Molnar. She was a much older teacher, probably somewhere close to her sixties. Her thinning hair was dyed jet black. She smiled when I walked into the class. Whether her smile was phony or not, it took some of the edge off my "what ifs."

It appeared that we could sit anywhere we wanted. I suppose it was only natural that I walked straight to the back of the room. I only waved to the students who waved at me. I had made up my mind to be like Cherry Gorden and not mix business with pleasure.

I thought I was doing fine until Arlene Thomas walked into the classroom. She greeted everyone as if she was part of the welcome committee. She finally spotted me and yelled my name. She acted as if she had not seen me in years. She ran to me like a happy little panting puppy. After hugging me she said, "I'm so glad you're in my class, Mona, aren't you?"

Trying not to let go of my pout I said, "Yeah!"

Again she said, "Mona, I'm so glad you're in my class!

"I'm glad too, Arlene."

Arlene knew what she was doing. She was trying to mess up my pretentious pout. She must have repeated herself at least ten times.

Since I wasn't returning the same energy, Arlene placed her pocketbook and notebook on a desk near mine and resumed socializing with the other students. I continued to sit and not let go of what I pretentiously held on to.

When the late bell rang, Mrs. Molnar asked everyone to have a seat. She introduced herself and then called the attendance.

I was really nervous. She had gefilte fish written all over her face. I knew I was headed for trouble if she was going to be anything like Miss Bliss.

There were thirty students. Eight were Afro Americans. Two of the eight I did not recognize.

Mrs. Molnar wanted us to be seated in alphabetical order. Right away murmuring went throughout the classroom. I did not want to be a part of the disruption because I knew that the ink pen she held in her hand had the power to repeat and the power to pass, and I certainly did not plan on repeating the sixth grade again!

My seating ended right in front of the teacher's desk. I had never sat that close to a teacher before. I felt like a catfish out of water.

Arlene sat two rows over and four seats back. Every now and then she'd press her lips together and send out a burst of air making that "Psst!" sound. Her mission was to get me to look back at her so that I could see her grin and wave. Arlene, of course, knew me too well. She knew that I loved to have fun;

therefore, I had to let go of my pretentious pout. Not only was she one of my cousins but we also went to the same church.

Arlene had a twin sister named Angela. We had all known each other since we were children. I had been with them long enough to tell them apart. Arlene had a squarer chin and a chicken pox scar on the side of her face. They both wore the same styled eyeglasses and yet I could easily tell them apart by looking at their eyes. Although both girls loved to play tricks and have fun, they also had different personalities. At church they both sang in the choir. Arlene sang alto and Angela sang soprano like P.J. and me.

At first I was embarrassed about being in that sixth-grade class, and then I realized that the only one who seemed bothered by it was me. Pouting was negative and made me feel like a real loser. I did not want to make things worse for myself than they already were. I had to move on and stop feeling sorry for myself. With eight Afro American students in my classroom, I had more going for me than against me.

I took my class work very seriously. I studied my notes as if my life depended on it. I did every homework assignment. The only grades I wanted to see on my papers were the passing ones.

Hallelujah! My prayers were answered. My brain finally opened like the Red Sea. I was no longer the dunce of the school. Daddy was right. I did have the ability to learn. It felt good. I was no longer academically challenged.

I scored an "A" on my first history test. Although I studied, I was still amazed that I passed that test. At first I thought Mrs. Molnar was trying to be nice, but then I realized that I earned that grade fair and square.

When Mrs. Molnar taught math it made sense. As long as I did my homework and made good grades, the outcome was always as good as going trick-or-treating. Clearly it was more rewarding to stay focused than to be stuck somewhere in La-La Land.

Our class performed in a play. I was part of a dance routine. Mrs. Molnar assigned me to choreograph the moves. My line was mute but so what; at least I was in the play. Arlene and the other soul sisters were in the routine too. Arranging that dance routine not only was an assignment in leadership, but it also helped me to feel good about myself.

Having Arlene as my classmate was truly a gift from God; I don't know how I would have managed if she was not in my class. How could I have kept a pout face with her around? Arlene's sense of humor certainly took the sting out of repeating that "purgatory" grade.

Mrs. Molnar was also an excellent teacher. She taught well and used her wisdom to help me rise to a new level. I felt confident. I didn't exactly fall in love with school, but at least I learned not to hate it. What I finally learned from having her for a teacher was that I shouldn't always judge a book by its cover.

Just when I thought I felt good about myself, my confidence was put to the test. On one particular day when walking home from school, P.J. and the rest of the gang slowed down to a few steps behind me. When I heard them giggling, I couldn't have been in La-La Land that long. I turned around to see what they were laughing about, and all they did was fling the backs of their fingers at me and urged me to turn around and keep on walking. Naturally I took offense. I was practically in tears. I thought they were talking about me! I couldn't believe how P.J. went along with them.

That following Saturday evening I looked out of the dining room window. I could not believe my eyes. Some of my school friends were going to P.J.'s house with gifts in their hands. I did not have a clue as to what was going on. When I asked Mommy about it, she said that P.J. decided to have a little party for one of her school friends. Of course I questioned her as to why I wasn't informed. Mommy's response was, "Oh, P.J. did invite you, but I must have forgotten to tell you. Didn't I tell you?"

"No! But when did she tell you, Mommy?"

"She told me when I was on the phone talking to your aunt, but when I got off the phone I must have gotten so busy that I forgot to tell you.'

I was so puzzled and hurt. How could P.J. not tell me herself? Having a party was considered massive no matter how small it was. Fortunately for P.J., my gullibility allowed me to quickly forgive her for not telling me personally about the party.

I tried to phone her, but her mother said she was busy. Trying to connect with her was like chasing a rainbow. I needed to know who the party was for. I couldn't take it anymore so I ran up the street to find her, but when I got to the front of her house I saw Rex Briggs. He looked at me as if he had seen a ghost.

"Where are you going? Who is that gift for?" I asked.

He never answered me. All he did was bounce his head up and down and from left to right. I felt as if I was in some Twilight Zone. How come everyone knew about this party except me? I still wanted to talk to P.J., but now all her guests were showing up.

I didn't want to stand there and just be a spectator. Instead of wasting time I decided to go back home and get dressed. I wore my Easter dress. It was the newest dress I had. It was pink and made of chiffon. From shoulder to waist the dress was body formed. Its sash was velvet and its skirt was fluffy. I had just received my first pair of nylon stockings for my thirteenth birthday. It was a gift from P.J.'s mom. I nearly fainted after opening that gift! It was the only thing I really wanted for my birthday and now this was my opportunity to wear them.

It seemed I couldn't walk fast enough in my Queen Anne heels. I was so worried about how I looked. Not having an invitation was no longer an issue. The only important thing was to just get there.

When I rang her door bell, I did not hear any noise. When the door was opened I saw no activity. I kissed and greeted her mom. When I asked where P.J. was, my aunt sent me straight to the basement of the house.

It seemed strange that the lights were out. As soon as I called out for P.J., everyone yelled, "SURPRISE!" and "HAPPY BIRTHDAY!"

SEVENTH HEAVEN

When the unclean spirit is gone out of a man, he walks through dry places, seeking rest and finds none.

Then he says, I will return unto my house from whence I came out; and when he is come, he finds it empty, swept, and garnished.

Then go he and take with him seven other more wicked than himself, and they enter in and dwell there and the last state of that man is worse than the first.   Matthew 26:43-45

Figuratively speaking, seven is the number for completion. The cycle for one week is seven days. The seventh day is devoted to God. Some people thank their lucky stars—and the Big Dipper has seven of them. Some people believe ladybugs bring them good luck because each bug has seven spots. As for me, going to the seventh grade was like experiencing one of the seven wonders of the world.

For the first time in my life I was completely confident about learning my academics. I was hopeful. Miracles were naturally welcomed, but I learned that I couldn't just sit around and wait for lucky good grades to happen. The hurt and embarrassment of repeating the sixth grade still existed, but I did not let that steal all my joy.

I felt as if I was in seventh heaven because I was an official junior high school student. Being in the seventh grade gave me seven privileges: hall lockers, gym lockers, gym suits, curriculum choices, different teachers for each subject, changing classes, and study hall.

Changing classes was the best part about being in the seventh grade. It would have been even more exciting if P.J. was around. She had already graduated to the high school.

Most of my teachers were men. Thank God none of them were like Mr. Kleinberg. My science teacher was a very attractive man. His name was Mr. Miller.

One day during a class discussion he stressed the importance of getting proper sleep at night. I thought this might be an opportunity to share the symptoms of my sleeping problems. I was hoping to hear others share their similar experience. Instead, all I received were their deer-eyed stares. Mr. Miller also looked at me as if I was crazy. Everyone acted as if I was making it up. I couldn't believe that no one else experienced waking up and not being able to move. If Mr. Miller had done all of his homework, then he would have known what I was talking about and also would have found me to be an interesting case to study.

I actually enjoyed all of my classes. Although I did not sleep too much in class I still daydreamed. With discipline I trained myself to stay focused. My brother was one grade behind me and that was the way I intended to keep it.

Prejudice looked better when I wore my rose-colored glasses. Just because I could not change it did not mean that I would let it change me.

CHAPTER 18

THE SPIRIT OF '66

By the time I reached eighth grade, I had had enough of Fillmore Jr. High School. Six years of being stuck in the same school felt like purgatory. Graduating put an end to that torture. I was ready to move on to the next milestone.

I was only going to be a high school freshman, but it made me feel on top of the world. Daddy must have a felt the same way about himself—he was now answering his calling. That summer he began seminary training, and I was going to high school. Certainly it was a blessing to have a father that built an earthly home and who was now sending up more timbers to build his heavenly home.

The summer of 1966 was pretty redemptive for my dad. The maintenance on our family car was now starting to look bleak. No matter how many new parts Daddy put into fixing it, something else was always going wrong. No matter how much Mommy cleaned, the house reeked of the car's motor oil. He said that car was an example of putting new wine into old wine skins. Mommy did not appreciate where his hands had touched the doors and the walls, and his supervisor did not appreciate his tardiness or his absenteeism. He had done his best to keep that car running, but his best wasn't good enough anymore. Daddy didn't like seeing Mommy upset and he certainly did not want to jeopardize his job. After considering his problem long enough, he found a solution.

He purchased a new car. It was a win/win situation. He had to get a loan, but he didn't mind. Owning a brand-new car made Daddy very proud, but that did not mean that everyone else was very happy for him. A certain neighbor on Hickory Street, someone old enough to be his mother, gave Daddy some interesting advice. Her name was Mrs. Grady. One afternoon she walked over to our street and watched how happily Daddy washed his car. With a squeamish kind of look, she said, "Hey, Joel, is that your car?"

"Yes, Mrs. Grady, this is my car."

"Okay, now you got to pay for it!"

"Thanks, Mrs. Grady, but tell me something I don't already know."

At first Mrs. Grady's off-key comment took the grin right off Daddy's face. After saying what she had to say she immediately turned around and walked back up the road. Being the nice man he was, Daddy waited till she was out of hearing range, then all of a sudden he threw the wet rag down from his hand onto the hood of the car and shouted, "Sanballat!"

I had never heard that word before. My eyes must have been bigger than an owl's. I thought it was a new word to say when you were frustrated.

"Do you know who Sanballat is?" he asked.

Before I could answer he told me, "He was one of the men in the Bible who scornfully laughed at Nehemiah about rebuilding the wall of Jerusalem."

Often during seminary school Daddy would compare certain Biblical characters to the people he knew in his life. He went on to finish his point.

"Mrs. Grady used to be one of the people who came down this street just to tell me that this house would never get built. Now that I have this car, she'll be checking on me to see if I'll have to give it back."

It was a relief to see the smile return to Daddy's face. This was his first brand-new car and he was proud to have it. It was a wonder that Mrs. Grady did not spit on the ground. Her attitude taught me that just because people are older does not mean they are any wiser.

The first ride our family took in our 1966 Dodge Cornet was to Stony Brook. Daddy had planned to see one of his best friends. Pine Street was one of the streets that we passed before getting there. I asked Daddy to turn where we used to live.

"Daddy, can we ride down the street where we use to live?"

"What do you want to see down there?"

"I just want to see where we lived one more time, please?"

As Daddy drove down Pine Street, he reminisced about how he used to chop wood and buy coal to heat the iron stoves. He reminded us how he used to go to the ice house and purchase a big block of ice to keep the refrigerator cool. He laughed about the times he sent Mrs. Hawkins away by showing her his paid receipts.

While he talked, I tried to remember what the house looked liked inside. I tried to picture where I used to sleep and how the living room was arranged. I tried to remember how I used to play on that front porch. The more I tried to visualize each memory the harder it became to imagine ever living there. In those few moments it felt as if all my memories of that house had vanished.

Just as I did on the day we moved from "purgatory" Pine Street, I rose to my knees and looked out of the back window. As I looked back at the house, it seemed much smaller than I had remembered. It was just a shoe box compared to our home in Mulberry.

The tattered curtain from the front window was sheer enough to see a light bulb connected to its un-shaded lamp stand. The car that was parked across the grass gave the appearance that the house was occupied. Strangely, the aura of the house looked desolate. Perhaps it just was some of my own feelings that felt a little deserted.

There was something I needed to ask. The house was almost out of sight before I got off of my knees. I simply asked, "Daddy, whatever happened to Sandra?"

"Sam says she ran away shortly after we left. I heard that she married a guy who gets drunk. They say he beats her all the time."

My heart filled with the shadows of sadness as I listened to Sandra's unfortunate status. Sandra could not have been too much more than twenty-one years old. Mommy always told me there was safety in numbers, but where was Sandra's safety? Sandra had promised me that she was going to run away and now it looked as if she had run out of "purgatory" and into the fire. For her sake maybe she would run away again, but this time to a better life. In my heart I had hoped to see her green eyes again.

I was so preoccupied with thoughts about her that I did not realize we were at the home of Daddy's friend.

Mr. Parks also owned a house. Daddy had known him since I was a baby. He and his wife had seven sons. Their only daughter was a twin to one of them. They had always been like family to us. Also living with them was the sister of Daddy's friend.

Her name was Valerie. She was from New Orleans. She and I were the same age. Just recently she came to live with her brother because their mother had died. At the time Valerie had no one else to take care of her.

Valerie stood about one or two inches taller than me. Her eyes were mysterious and dark like charcoal and yet they also sparkled like diamonds. Her skin was also dark and pretty.

We talked about fashion and boys. I told her that I was looking forward to being a freshman in high school. I shared with her some of the fun adventures that I experienced when going on church outings.

As Valerie began to share with me the stories about her mother's death, I could have sworn I saw something dark like a shadow coming over her. The feeling I got was so strange. She told me that her mother died from someone putting roots on her. She said that her mother felt as if something was crawling in her body all the time. Valerie believed that a curse had killed her mother.

At that time the only roots I knew about were the roots in the ground and the roots in my hair and the square root of the number nine.

Valerie cocked her head to the side, twirled her fingers through the locks of her afro, and stared me in the face with squinted eyes. Then she said, "You don't really know what I'm talking about, do you?"

That evening Valerie introduced me to the knowledge of things that I had hoped to never experience. Whatever her assignment was in this life, it must have been to scare me. I often wonder what my life would have been like if we had never met.

"Mona, do you believe in spirits?"

When she asked me that, the spear of fear went right inside my heart.

"What kind of spirits, Valerie?"

The only spirit I was willing to talk about was the Holy Spirit. I wasn't about to share with her the footsteps I had heard at night at my grandparents' home. There was something about Valerie's eyes which made me feel she came from a darker world. As she continued to twirl her fingers through her hair, she also continued to gaze at me as if she could see through me. Finally she shook her head as if she was in disbelief.

"Don't you know? Haven't you heard of the kind of spirits that people see when they have been born with a veil over their face?"

Gathering from the look on her face, she was trying to size me up, and gathering from the look on my face, Valerie knew that I did not have a clue as to what she was talking about. What she said really gave me the creeps. I did not like where this was going and now a little peer pressure was starting to weave in. I didn't want Valerie to think I was a scaredy-cat. What she said sounded crazy, but I also had a feeling that it could be true, but why was she telling me all of this! The only veils I knew about were wedding veils, and as far as I knew, babies did not get married.

"Born with a veil? I never heard of that."

While trying to be respectful, I foolishly listened to what she had to say.

"You don't know what a veil is? It's a layer of extra skin found over the face on newborn babies. When that happens, they see spirits."

Now I was really beginning to feel uneasy and I did not want to talk about spirits anymore. I had not felt that uncomfortable since the days of the *Bogey-Man*.

She went on to say, "One of my cousins was born with a veil over her face and she sees spirits all the time."

"Is she the only one that can see them?" I asked.

"Yeah, sometimes she sees a circus of animals. One of the animals is like her pet. It's a dog. She calls him Silver because beautiful silvers of light shine at the end of each one of his hairs."

Every so often she would shift her eyes to the side as if seeing something that only she could see. She also said that her cousin could see a "Slave Boy" who was her spirit guide and also her messenger. She claimed that her cousin could hear the chains of the "Slave Boy" rattling a mile away.

Valerie was scary. I'm sure she smelled the fear that ranked all over me. I didn't know about "roots," I had never heard about "veils," and I certainly did not want to know about spirit guides. The only spirit guide I needed was the Holy Spirit. Clayton helped me out also, but Valerie didn't need to know about him.

I suspect it was Valerie who saw those spirits. I tried to act impressed as she babbled on about the different spirits that visited her cousin. Each story she told seemed to birth more fear in my own spirit. I never should have asked Daddy to drive through "purgatory" Pine Street. Perhaps it was fate. After all, wasn't that the place where my fears were born?

Normally I didn't like to leave early when we visited with family and friends. In this case, I was ready to leave ASAP.

I believed that Valerie had her own set of spirits and I did not want them imposed upon me. I had my own problems. Wasn't the *Witch* enough? I always wished I had someone other than Mommy to talk to about the *Witch* and I was sure Valerie would have been interested, but at that point I just wanted to leave.

The night had already fallen. I wanted to get away from her. I suggested that we go in the house. When I saw my parents, I pretended to look sleepy. Finally Daddy said, "Let's go!" I was careful to not let Valerie catch me alone so I walked between my father and mother as they walked to the car.

On the way home, I asked my parents if there was any such thing as babies being born with a veil over their eyes. I was so sorry I asked. Daddy said that he was born with that skin over his face. He said as a child he saw spirits all the time. Mommy advised me not to follow bouncing lights because it usually led to death.

My parents explained that if I ever saw a spirit, I should ask it, "What do you want?" They claimed that the spirits would have to answer or go away, but in my heart I knew if I saw a spirit, I would be the one running away. My parents also said that spirits could reveal themselves through drugs and alcohol. They said that was why alcohol was also called "spirits."

Mommy said angels in heaven were spirits. Daddy said the devil was a spirit and he had his own army of demons. They said either way we were surrounded by them all the time.

The rest of the ride home went something like the ride home when we were on vacation. Daddy went on and on about the spirits he had seen in the past. I did not want to hear any more stories about spirits. There was nowhere to escape in that car. Again I had no choice but to listen to the gobbledygook about spirits all the way home.

I was so glad when Daddy finally drove into the driveway. I didn't think my body would ever stop shaking. My head was filled with Valerie stories, Daddy stories, and Mommy stories and yet they did not know about my story. All I ever wanted was a true explanation as to how to make the *Witch* go away.

That night I slept with the light in my bedroom on. Thanks to Trinity Baptist Sunday School for giving me my first New Testament Bible. It was a gift for graduating from the eighth grade. I kept my little Bible in the upper part of my pajamas close to my heart. The *Witch* didn't bother me because I was too afraid to go to sleep. I may have tossed and turned all night, but like a vampire at the crack of dawn, I finally fell into a deep sleep.

The summer of '66 was not too much different than any other summer. Daddy was eager to go south in his new car. He said that was one good way to break it in. It was not air conditioned but at least it was dependable.

My grandparents lived in the South. My father's parents lived in North Carolina and my mother's mom lived in Georgia. Both grandparents on each side owned ranch-style homes. Each home had a tin roof, a living room, two bedrooms, one kitchen, one bath, and a front and back porch. Neither home had an attic, basement, or hallway. The first half of our vacation we stayed in North Carolina with Daddy's parents, Granddaddy Jack and Grandma Hattie. The second part of our vacation we spent in Georgia with Mommy's mom, Grandma Lottie. It was such a joy to see Granddaddy Jack and Grandma Hattie, but on that first night, *déjà vu*. Winky and I slept in that front room again and all night long, that spirit walked from one side of the room to the other. The *Witch* visited me at least three times. I didn't bother telling anyone about the visitations. For the rest of the week I asked to sleep at the home of my other dear cousins.

After leaving North Carolina, we visited Georgia to see Grandma Lottie. I was also happy to arrive there. I had many cousins that lived in her home town and I couldn't wait to see them. Hanging over the inside front door of Grandma Lottie's house was a horseshoe. I asked her about that horseshoe but Mommy answered and said it was for good luck. Grandma shook her head and looked at Mommy from the corner of her eyes and said that the house used to belong to her in-laws and they nailed that horseshoe there to keep the *Witches* and the *Devils* away. I wanted to ask more questions, but Mommy changed the subject. Grandma Lottie also had a portrait of a beautiful colored "Guardian Angel" that hung on the wall in her living room. In the painting were two other colored children crossing an unsecured bridge built over a dangerous stream of water. The painting always reminded me of Winky and me.

Grandma Lottie was amazing. She was well into her fifties and had a nice-sized vegetable garden and walked over a mile to work. Although Grandma didn't have a driver's license at the time, she did not have to walk anywhere. Half the town knew her. Grandma had lots of superstitions and I think she trusted riding with the white folks she worked for better than most of the people of her own color. She always walked to and from work with an umbrella over her head. The Georgia sun was hot and Grandma was also conscious of curses that might be hanging somewhere in a tree. She suspected that sometimes we could catch a curse that was meant for someone else.

During our visit my parents slept in the guest bedroom. Winky slept in the living room and I slept in the room with my grandmother. Her bed was across from mine. The kitchen window was straight across the room from where I slept. When her bedroom light went out, there was nothing left to see. The room was pitch black. When my eyes adjusted, I was able to see the illumination of green numbers that glowed from Grandma's clock.

According to that clock, five minutes had gone by. It seemed like a very long five minutes because I heard every tick and every tock. The clock sounded as if it had a microphone attached to it. My grandmother wound the clock every night before going to bed and now the clock was winding me. On that first night I knew it was going to be rough. Not only could I not block out the sound of the clock, the crickets and the frogs also had an annoying melody of their own. The way my grandmother was breathing told me that she was fast asleep. It seemed as if everyone was sleeping except me. How could I sleep with all those sounds orchestrating in my ears?

The light that illuminated from my grandmother's alarm clock had finally lost its final glow. Much of the snoring had also simmered down to a mere purr. Still, I wasn't asleep. The night was not only long, but the morning seemed light years away. Just when I was about to doze, I sensed something bright that went across my eyelids.

My first thought was that it must have been the headlights of a passing car, but I didn't hear any motor. My second thought was that it must have been someone walking with a flashlight. That seemed reasonable enough until I realized the light was shining from inside the kitchen window. I tried to adjust my eyes by rubbing them, but all I saw was a big circle of light. It felt like a big eyeball was staring at me. That light was the only thing I could see. My heart was the only thing I could now hear. I wanted that light to go away. I got the impression that it was trying to connect to me, but I didn't want to connect with it. Other than itself, the light revealed nothing, not even a shadow. I was alarmed. Nothing else seemed to exist except my hammering heart and that circle of light.

I was able to move and I wanted to scream, but I was too afraid. How could I be sure if it was a spirit or a Peeping Tom? The one thing I knew for sure was that I wanted it to go away.

If this was the light that Mommy talked about, then I was going to fight it all the way. I didn't want to die and go to that light. My heart already felt as if it was going to give way. Something within me told me to keep still, and that is exactly what I did. I had heard that internal voice before. The light seemed to stay there forever. What more did I have to lose? Without moving a muscle, I tightly closed my eyes and pretended to be asleep. I don't think fainting would have been harmful, but I did my best to keep strong so that I would not find myself a victim of that light.

The following morning I told my grandmother and my parents about that light. Mommy said it was probably a Peeping Tom. I didn't think it was a Peeping Tom and I certainly wasn't going to bother to debate. Any other explanation would have been more than I could handle. Strangely, later that day the house smelled like sulfur had been burned. When I questioned my mother about what I smelled, she looked at me and held the palm of her hand in my face to indicate for me not to ask any more questions.

CHAPTER 19

PHONE-E

Marilyn Monroe sang that diamonds are a girl's best friend, but to a teenage girl the telephone is a girl's best friend. Mommy felt that I spent too much time on the phone. An hour on the phone always seemed like only a few minutes. While growing into my teen years I began to see a side to my dad that I never knew existed. He had always been my hero and always will be, but when I was a teenager Daddy was strict and over-protective.

When I was fourteen years of age, I met a young man at church equivalent to my age. He lived about two towns away. We exchanged phone calls and letters. We fell in love. He wanted to visit me and I felt likewise.

At this point I had never dated, so I asked for permission. I was on my way to high school where I would have been if it had not been for Mr. Kleinberg. Shouldn't that have counted for something?

At first I asked my mother for permission. "Mommy, Sidney wants to come and visit me on Saturday. Can he come over?"

"I don't think you're old enough. You'll have to ask your father."

When Daddy came home from work, I waited till we had dinner and then I asked, "Daddy, can Sidney come over?"

"No."

"Why?"

"You're not old enough."

"I am fourteen years old, Daddy. Why can't I see him?"

"What did I say? I am not going to repeat myself."

"Can he come over for about an hour?"

The look in Daddy's eyes told me to back off. As a little girl, I didn't remember his denials being so mean.

Sidney and I dated over the phone. It was cool for a while. As time went by, he apparently felt as though our phone dates were as good as "phony bologna." I could not blame Sidney for wanting to move on. It broke my heart, but it was fun while it lasted.

In our circle of school friends some of us needed a little attitude adjustment. A lot of us were two-faced, others were phony, and a few even thought too highly of themselves.

To stop some of the madness, we all agreed to make a truce. We took an autograph book and turned it into a slam book. Each page was dedicated to at least one person. It was passed from person to person. The positives comments were always acceptable, but the negative ones usually triggered anger and then ended in some kind of physical altercation. These matters were usually settled by the railroad tracks or a block away from school.

Obviously our slam book was not a very good idea. Yes, we made a truce, but none of us were mature enough to handle each other's constructive criticism. My parents always taught me to not say anything if I did not have anything nice to say. As a teenager it was sometimes hard to look neutral without looking two-faced.

Most of my female friends had boyfriends at school. There was always someone either breaking up or making up. I did not care for all that kind of drama. I kept my relationships neutral. It wasn't that I did not like any of the guys; I just wanted to keep it safe. Confrontations could be embarrassing. Mulberry was too small for comfort. Sometimes playing it safe could be mistaken for being arrogant. If the guys in Mulberry felt that I was a phony, I am sure they got over it.

YOUTH REVIVAL

Coming to Mulberry High School was very special to me. It meant reuniting with my cousin P.J. Even though she had only two years to graduate, I still was grateful to be with her in high school.

P.J. was a number-one model student. Not only did she make honor roll, but she was also still very good at doing forward rolls and backward rolls. Every tumble she did, she did smoothly. P.J. always wanted to be a cheerleader at school, but the little glitch was that Mulberry High School had never had an Afro American cheerleader. Of course she did not let that stop her. P.J. said her mother always encouraged her to shoot for the stars. Keeping that in mind, she signed up for the tryouts.

I was so proud of her! I am sure everyone else felt the same. I heard that she was one of the best cheerleaders ever. I saw her at practice, but I only made it to a couple of games. I should have made it my business to be there for her. How could I ever make it up to her? The games were always on Saturday mornings. I would have loved to have seen her cheerleading, but my best sleep always came after daybreak. Saturday morning was the only day of the week that I could catch up on my best sleep. Most nights I did not sleep too well. P.J. had sweet dreams and I had nightmares.

In the autumn of 1967 a twelve-year-old evangelist preached for one week for a youth revival at Trinity Baptist. His name was Darren Boyd.

When Evangelist Darren preached, all the youth, and especially the teens of the church, responded like the people on the day of Pentecost. For the first two nights he preached, Terry and I sat back like spectators watching P.J., Arlene, and Angela as they jumped up and down at the altar call, but on that third night, I decided to go to the altar call. Terry had a smirk written all over her face but I didn't care. I could not control myself anymore. My body felt as if it was on fire. I jumped up and down and spun in circles. No, I wasn't exactly doing cartwheels, but it sure felt like it. I screamed and cried till my body shook all over. Heavenly language poured out of my mouth as if it were my native tongue. My soul felt so close to God that night that I practically wanted Him to take my soul right then and there. I figured if He took my soul in that very hour then I would have a fairer chance of making it above the clouds without being in an airplane.

A jubilant mania swept from one teen to the next teen. Our parents and ushers were overwhelmed. They could not contain us, control us, or calm us down. That was one week the ushers almost turned into bouncers.

After youth revival week I hungered to know more about the B-I-B-L-E. After all, the acronyms stand for Believers' Instructions Before Leaving Earth. I read all of Matthew, Mark, Luke, and John. I tried to memorize a few verses. What I read and what I understood were two different things. I finally came to an understanding that some lessons came with time, others with wisdom, and the rest with hard knocks.

CHAPTER 20

SILENT PROTEST

On April 4, 1968, in my ninth-grade year, our Nobel Peace Prize leader of civil rights was assassinated. This tragedy felt like the end of the world. Although his life ended on the balcony of a motel in Memphis, his memory and his dreams will always stay alive on the balcony of my heart.

Although Memphis is approximately six hundred miles from Mulberry, the event of his assassination felt as if it happened right around the corner in my home town.

The Afro American students of Mulberry High School made a pact to stay home from school on the day of his funeral. I thought that was the least we could do to show our respect. I did not expect my parents to disagree, but they did.

The more I begged to stay home from school the more they stood their ground. My heart was so heavy. I didn't want to be the only "black dot" in school that day.

Playing hooky crossed my mind, but the stakes were too high. It wouldn't have been that bad if getting suspended was my only problem; after all, didn't he go to jail for us? My parents had their own scared straight program. They said that I wasn't too old to get spanked with the belt; besides, I didn't want to be grounded for the rest of my life.

What choice did I have? The whole dilemma made me feel like a traitor. Even though I made the decision to be a good little lamb and go to school, I felt like a worthless scapegoat.

To be the only Afro American in school on the day of our civil rights leader's funeral was no more than a "judgment day" for me.

The night before "judgment day" I needed to consecrate myself. It was essential that I represented my people right. Just because I was going to be the only "black dot" in school didn't mean I was a traitor. Nor did it mean that I was ashamed of my color. I had no reason to be ashamed except that my parents were making me do something I didn't want to do.

Granted, when I was in grammar school, my classmates tried to make me ashamed of my color. I always wanted to fit in with everyone, but now I was beginning to realize that fitting in with everyone was just plain impossible. So what if my hair wasn't naturally straight; at least I had hair. I was pretty sure by now that the only person who had a problem with my forehead was me. There was no reason for me to be ashamed and I was tired of it. To be the only "black dot" in school felt scary, but I had to find a way to be brave. The bravest way to express myself was to cut my hair short. So...I washed it and gave it a 'fro. It was kind of a Joan of Arc thing.

When I went to sleep that night, I dreamed that I was late for school. When I walked into the classroom I instantly became the laughing stock. I was the only black student in the class. Everyone including the teacher laughed at my hair. When I changed classes I was laughed at. In spite of all the mockery, I walked with my head held high. It was one rough night. If I wasn't dreaming then I was fighting the *Witch*.

In my final dream that night, I dreamt that my cousin P.J. and the rest of our friends caught me going to school in spite of our pact. Everyone who saw me yelled, "Traitor!" P.J. on the other hand yelled, "When are you going to stand up for yourself?"

I was eager to get out of bed for two reasons. I needed time to shape my afro and needed to get up early before P.J. and our friends saw me walking to school.

It must have taken me forty-five minutes to get my hair right. I had to pick it, fluff it, and evenly pat it down. Mommy opened my bedroom door as if she was going to catch me doing something I wasn't supposed to do. The look on her face told me that she was angry more than she was shocked. With one of her hands on the door knob and the other on her hip she said, "I dreamed you cut your hair! What did you do that for? Why are wearing you hair like that?"

I answered by hunching my shoulders into the air. Personally I could have cared less about what she dreamed that night; thanks to her, I had nightmares too. Did she have any idea what I was going to be faced with or did she care?

In my first-period class I purposely sat in the first seat in the second row. Sitting there made it easy for me not to see, hear, or say anything to any soul. The only way I could bury my face in the sand without looking too obvious was to rest my elbows on the desk, bring my forearms to my face, and put my face in my hands.

My teacher, Mr. Von Goton, gave supportive remarks about the sad event on that day. I tried to hold back my tears because I didn't want him to think it was his remarks that touched me. I sat in the front row so I didn't have to look at my classmates. I am sure Mr. Von Goton didn't feel sorry for me, but the tears that fell from my eyes must have been too distracting to him. He asked me if I was alright. I nodded my head up and down to let him know I was okay. He gave me permission to leave the classroom, but I wouldn't.

Being that I was the only "black dot" in his classroom that day, I suspiciously thought that he wanted me out of his classroom. Why was he trying to be so nice and why was he trying to get me to leave the class? Perhaps as the only Afro American student in his class that day I was messing up his format.

I was not going to leave that class to give him the opportunity to talk about me behind my back or give him a chance to talk evil about our civil rights leader. Therefore, I did what I had to do. I took some tissue from my purse, wiped my nose, and put my tears in check.

Midway through the class, each student was asked to express how they felt about the events that led to that sad day. Many heartwarming remarks were expressed by all my classmates. When I was asked how I felt, I wanted to get indignant and ask Mr. Von Goton, "HOW DO YOU THINK I FEEL?" Instead I just sat there and shook my head from side to side to let him know I did not want to make a comment. I did not trust him; therefore, why should I give him a reason to gloat over the loss of my leader and over my grief?

Mr. Von Goton was persistent. All I could say was, "I am glad that he got to express his dream before he was killed. His dreams are also my dreams and I believe that one day God will bring it all to pass."

As the day progressed I received many acknowledgements from many of my fellow students, including the ones in the tenth, eleventh, and twelfth grades. Most of them had always walked past me without looking my way. Needless to say I remained guarded, but inwardly I was really touched by their concern.

Over and over my afro was complimented. A few exchange students offered their sincere condolences. I responded inherently as if I, Mona Cartman, was personally related or connected to my assassinated leader.

Things happened for a reason. It took the whole day for me to realize that I was more than just a representation of a "black dot" in the school. Moreover, I was a constant reminder of what that day was all about. At first I felt like a traitor, but silent protest turned out to be my tribute. To be in a school like Mulberry was part of the fulfillment of our civil rights leader's dream.

Mommy once told me if I wanted people to accept me, then I would have to also accept myself. For many years I felt ashamed because I thought my hair line metered my intelligence. After observing the intelligence of others, I finally realized that the perimeters of their hair line did not limit what was in their brains.

For many years I felt inferior, especially when I was amongst the whites. I chose to no longer feel that way. They might not have liked it, but I was also part of the fabric they were woven on. It took a long time coming, but I was no longer ashamed. Finally I could proudly say, "I am Black and I am proud."

DREAMLAND

In 1968, one of my father's brothers had a heart attack. When I went to visit him at the hospital, he told me that during his heart attack he had a near-death experience. He talked about how his spirit was lifted out of his body and taken way above the clouds. He said he was surrounded by lots of light, and everything was so peaceful. He said that he was ready to stay, but a voice told him that it was not his time, and after that he was sent back into his body.

My goodness, what was with all these stories about light? All my life I had been afraid of the dark. Now I was beginning to believe that light had a power of its own.

Mommy said to never follow the path of a mysterious light. The light I saw in 1966 at my grandmother's house will always remain a mystery. The Bible says that Jesus is light. I believe that the light my uncle saw must have been Jesus.

One of the most beautiful lights to see is the sun rising in the morning. Too bad for me, the only time I got to see that show was when we were on the road during vacation.

A restful night for me was a dream yet to come true. Constant visitations from the *Witch* always left me exhausted. How could I ever feel revived? Since waking up in the morning was always a chore, I vowed to myself that when I got out of high school I would get a nighttime job.

When Mommy slept she often had dreams that gave her a sneak preview of future events. One night she dreamt that three of Daddy's family members were fishing on a pier. Each one fell in the water one at a time. It took a space of about three years, but each one died in the order that she dreamed.

In 1969, when I was seventeen, I dreamed that I was at a carnival. It was a cloudy day. In the midst of the carnival was a king cobra. It stood at least ten feet tall. He stared at me with his fiery eyes. Behind his head was a black whirlwind.

I was disturbed by the dream and shared it with my mother. She confirmed that it meant trouble. She told me not to do anything to make my father upset.

Three months later the dream materialized. One evening, I left my pocketbook partly opened on the edge of my bed. Apparently it fell to the floor and exposed my cigarette. Unfortunately it was Daddy who discovered it and he was furious. He came at me as if he was going to kill me. The fire in his eyes was enough to light a whole carton of cigarettes.

What started out to be a beautiful day was one of the worst days of my life. The windows to my bedroom were raised and so was Daddy's voice. It was hard to keep silent when the hide of his belt continually connected to mine. You can bet that everyone in our neighborhood heard the news firsthand.

Earnestly I tried to explain that the cigarette did not belong to me, but as it turned out, it was my unlucky day!

Based on what I dreamt, the king cobra was Daddy. Its fiery stare was the flames I saw in my father's eyes. The whirlwind was his belt and the clouds were the smoke from the cigarette. The carnival was our curious neighbors.

To be honest, the cigarette was only a prop. I used it to look cool. Daddy didn't have anything to worry about. I never did like cigarettes. And of course after that I hated them.

That was one painful experience. I can't say that I wasn't forewarned. My question was how could seeing events of the future become an advantage if I didn't know what the signs were? To dream is one thing. To interpret it is another. No insight to the foresight can consequently lead to hindsight.

CHAPTER 21

BLIND DATE

It was the year 1969. I was about to be a junior in high school and P.J. was on her way to her first semester in college. We had recently received our driver's permits and P.J.'s father had recently purchased a brand new Oldsmobile deuce and a quarter. The exterior of the car was white and its interior was red. It also had a convertible top. When P.J. passed her driver's license test, she celebrated the cause by driving her father's new car every chance she could. When P.J. drove her father's three hundred-horse-powered engine, she looked like a royal princess on a white horse. To showboat, she wore her red wide-brimmed hat. The best part about when she drove her father's car was that I was usually with her.

The night before she went to college, we went on a double date with her boyfriend that lived in North Ever Wood. He arranged for me to be with his friend and we agreed to meet them at a party.

The party was held at the youth center in her boyfriend's home town. Before heading out to the party, P.J. suggested that we take one last drive around the town. As we cruised, her eyes began to fill with tears. The wind may have been one factor, but she was already getting homesick.

Going away to college meant being away from both her parents. P.J. was their only child. She had never been away from her mother. Periodically her father drove across the States in his tractor trailer. For the first time in her life she would be on her own.

Airfare was only nineteen dollars, but that didn't mean she was coming home every weekend. Her boyfriend from North Ever Wood didn't really want her to go. Anyway, what did he have to offer her? Going to college was her dream and the ticket to her future!

For her, college life had an itinerary of its own. Everyone knows that college is a whole new life filled with term papers, parties, and sporting events. The anticipation of being two hundred and fifty miles away from home was painful, but in the meantime it was...

Party time! It was time to meet the guys. P.J. parked the car, secured the top, and locked the doors. In North Ever Wood word got around quick. Before we could get to the party entrance, we were greeted by her boyfriend and his friend.

Without waiting to be introduced, his friend introduced himself to me. After he asked me for my name, he reached into the back pocket of his pants and pulled out a brown paper bag. It was a fifth of whisky. The seal had already been broken. He offered me a sip but I refused. After swigging a sizable amount, he wiped his lips and offered to escort me into the party.

I barely got a good look at his face. One of the street lights had been knocked out. It was just as dark inside the party as it was outside. Although the music was rocking and the party was hopping, the guys wanted to leave, especially after that third slow jam. P.J.'s boyfriend said that he really needed to talk with her. I wasn't ready to leave, but for now, where P.J. went...I went.

The guys wanted to take a little walk, but P.J. did not want to leave her father's car. She was going to put the convertible top back down but her boyfriend told her to leave it up. The interior lights of the car gave me some idea of what this blind date looked like. He wasn't a bad-looking man, but his face and his eyes mirrored the essence of his rough environment.

After riding through this town and that town we decided to hang out in a nearby park. The music from the eight-track cassette sounded romantic. My blind date eased his arm around my shoulder. He complimented my hair, my face, and the way I was dressed, but his whisky and cigarette breath made his moves less charming.

P.J. was already wiping her eyes and blowing her nose. She sobbed as if it was the end of the world. I suppose this new transition in her life was similar to taking the bitter with the sweet.

My blind date suggested that we get out of the car to give P.J. and her boyfriend a little privacy. He claimed he needed to stretch his legs. Judging from the way he looked at me, that was not the only thing he wanted to stretch.

When I got out of the car, P.J. recommended that I stay close by. I assured her I would. However, as we talked, we walked in circles around the car. The perimeters of our walk began to widen like a loosened coil. He pointed to a nearby sandbox and suggested we take a seat.

After we sat down, I wondered if that was part of his plan. He did most of the talking, constantly expressing the attraction he had for me.

Each time I questioned him about him or his family he would get quiet or respond by hunching his shoulders. I couldn't imagine why he did not want to talk about himself or his family. The only thing I knew about him was his name and where he was from.

It was dark, the moon was full, and the nearest street light was too far away. I began to feel uneasy. When I rose to my feet, he also stood. He became aggressive and reached for my arms, making it impossible for me to get away. His language began to get vulgar. He was like a dragon. His breath not only reflected what he drank, but it also felt hot and disgusting on my neck.

He had the audacity to say that a girl like me needed a man like him. After he said that he licked the side of my face like a dog. He forced me down on the seat of the sandbox. I managed to elbow him in his side. It must have really angered him because he took hold of the sleeve on my brand-new satin purple blouse and ripped it right off my shoulder.

It was time to call for help. After I yelled for P.J., he placed his hand over my mouth. That really caught me off guard. His hand felt as if it was going to suffocate me. He told me to keep still. When he saw that P.J. did not respond, he pushed me down to the middle of the sandbox. Before I could rise to my feet he was on top of me. He began to pull at my hair with one hand and with the other hand he managed to yank off every piece of elastic that I had around my waist.

His strength was unnatural. I begged for him to stop. I could not believe he had gone that far. He was out of control! He shamelessly exchanged his pleasure for my pain. Who was this guy? I feared for my life. As bad as I wanted to scream, I couldn't. I was afraid he would suffocate me with his hand or choke me. While he continued to force himself on me, I closed my eyes and prayed that he would one day suffer for what he was doing.

I also prayed that P.J. would be alright. There was only a few more hours left before we'd say good-bye. When she goes to college...

During the time when I was thinking about P.J., I could feel myself being separated from my body. I felt the presence of someone that I had not been with for a long time. I was taken away. I saw myself walking on the campus of a large college. Many students black and white waved at me. Ahead of me was a big white building that looked like a court house. I did not want to stop walking, but a chilling voice came to my ear.

"How did it feel?"

It sounded familiar. When I opened my eyes it was as if I was sent right back into my body. Hearing this voice was a nightmare.

Still pulling at my hair he insisted that I give him an answer.

"HOW DID IT FEEL?"

What did he expect me to say? He was tearing my hair out of my head. He had forced himself upon me. The weight of his body upon me made it harder for me to breathe. I was glad to still be alive. It felt as if I was practically buried in the sand and then he said it again.

"HOW DID IT FEEL?"

He was demanding an answer. Certainly I wasn't going to give him something he wanted to hear. After what he did to me it was time for his ego to be raped.

"What are you talking about? What did you do? Feel what? I didn't feel anything."

"What do you mean you didn't feel anything?"

Bingo! What I said must have struck a nerve.

He took a handful of my hair and yanked it out! He raised the upper part of body and hit me hard on my head. I saw a galaxy of stars that didn't come from the sky. Finally he got completely off of me. When he stood up, he took his shoe and kicked sand into my face. It was already dark and I couldn't see, and now I was also blinded by the sand.

Getting my hair pulled out from the roots and getting sand kicked into my eyes hurt too, but it also felt good to know that I had hurt his pride. Telling him something other than what he thought he was going to hear might have been foolish, but I felt I had to do it.

What kind of blind date was this? Momentarily I was blinded by the sand and also seeing stars! When my eyes began to focus, I looked to the sky and saw the real stars. What had happened to me was unfortunate, but at least I was still alive.

What was left of my hair, I couldn't imagine. My clothes were torn and I was a mess. I tried to straighten myself the best I could. I needed to get back to P.J....

As I walked I looked to the sky and thanked God for being alive. Maybe it was just my imagination, but as I walked, the stars seemed to twinkle back at me. Each sparkle was like seeing a miracle. Each twinkle showed me goodness and also showed me mercy. I knew that God was watching and I knew it was His angels that saved me.

When I got back to the car all I wanted to do was go home. I felt nasty and my body ached. My hair, my body, my clothes, and my shoes were full of sand.

When I got into the car I could hear P.J. sniffle her nose. I told her I was ready. Her boyfriend drove the car back to the party. No one said a word. It was like riding in a funeral car. I just wanted this night to end.

After the guys got out of the car, I couldn't wait to tell P.J. what that guy did. She looked as if she almost wanted to hit me.

"Didn't I tell you not to go far? Why didn't you stay by the car?"

"I didn't realize I was that far from the car and when I did he wouldn't let me come back. I had no idea it would end up like this. I hate him!"

"What do you want to do? Do you want to report him?"

"You know I can't do that. Daddy would be so mad he would probably try to kill him and then kill me for going out with someone I didn't even know."

"Do you think you'll be alright?"

"I'll be alright, what can I do? P.J., this is your night. I don't want to ruin it.

We cried all the way home.

From the moment I met that guy, I should have seen the red flag. This blind date was not much of a gentleman. He had already started drinking before we met. Instead of waiting to be introduced he abruptly introduced himself. Swigging from the bottle was unethical; to not flinch meant that he was a pro.

We should have never left that party. I should have never wandered away from the car. I hate to admit it, but Mommy was right. There is safety in numbers, but this was one number I didn't see coming.

I decided I would never tell my parents about that night. The results would not have been favorable for the offender or me. He would have gone to jail and I would have been grounded for life.

That particular night was one eerie ordeal. My blind date was an actual paradigm of all my fears. He was the *Sand-Man*, *Bogey-Man,* and the *Witch* all rolled into one.

Normally the sandbox is an innocent place to play. For me it was the place where my innocence was taken away.

Hindsight is frustrating. That ordeal made me learn what to keep in mind on my next date. Clayton promised me that I would never be a victim of that kind of crime again. I believed him, and that was what gave me hope.

When P.J. went to college, I missed her dearly. We wrote each other all the time. I am sure my misspelled words kept her laughing. She had always been the one with the brains. It was all good because whatever I needed to know I would ask her.

P.J. was more than just a cousin to me. She was my confidante. We had shared things we would take only to our graves. She would always be my gift from God.

Seeing her during the Thanksgiving holiday was like having Christmas again. We celebrated her homecoming by cruising all over town in her dad's car.

It was Black Friday, the Friday after Thanksgiving. P.J. wanted to surprise her boyfriend, so she and I took a ride out to North Ever Wood to find him. Surprising him was usually hard. In the projects, news got around fast. That deuce and a quarter was a beauty and everyone knew who it belonged to.

Geographically, to get to the projects, we had to pass the North Ever Wood Teen Center. The teen center was only a few feet ahead, but the street was filled with teens and cars. It was unusually noisy. In order for her to drive by, P.J. had to really ease up on her speed. As she drove through the street the crowd began to part like the Red Sea. We could see P.J.'s boyfriend in the midst of it. As he walked toward us we could see that he was also trying to flag us down.

Beyond him a man was on the ground. It appeared that he had been slain. As P.J.'s boyfriend got closer she rolled her window down to greet him. Anguish was all over his face. He breathed heavily with worry. Perspiration ran down his face and neck, and the front of his shirt was torn.

"Go back, P.J.! Go back! My boys are out here fighting! I don't want you hurt. Baby, just go! Get out of here before the police come."

Before going back to battle, he gave her a kiss. P.J. held on to his arm and told him to be careful, but before he left, she asked, "Who is that lying on the ground?" When P.J. and I heard him say the name, we nearly froze. I don't know what ran through her mind, but "Black Jack" is what ran through mine. This night was a winner.

P.J.'s mission that night was to surprise her boyfriend. It was one of those nights full of surprises, especially for the person lying on the ground. Again this was supposed to be P.J.'s night, but now it felt as if it was my night!

On the evening of the next day I went to P.J.'s house to visit. The telephone rang. It was her boyfriend. Her conversation went something like this: "Hello. Yeah, this is P.J. What do you mean? Why do you want me to stay away? Is it really that bad out there? How bad did he get hurt? How many stitches did he get on his neck? Twenty-one stitches! Wow! Is he still in the hospital? When can I see you again?"

P.J. hung up the phone and cried. She felt his love slipping away. I believe he wanted the best for her and he was not it. His future was shallow. Every time he'd shoot for something it would hit the ceiling and come back. On the other hand, P.J. was full of hope. She was always shooting for the stars. Theoretically they both had high hopes, but it was for a different purpose.

I didn't feel sorry for his partner. He was lucky God spared his life. I continued to trust God for what I witnessed and my peace was finally restored.

Cherry lost academic credits on account of her multiple psychiatric hospitalizations. We shared many of the same classes. English literature was one of them.

The English Literature Department scheduled a field trip to see the movie *Romeo and Juliet*. The Ever Wood Cinema Theater was within walking distance. It was outside of Mulberry, located at the new mall.

After arriving at the theater Cherry and I used the bathroom. I had been cramping. I stood over the commode. As soon as I removed my napkin, something plopped into the toilet bowl. It looked like a red ball. I screamed. I didn't know what it was. I started to run out of the stall, but my bottom half was exposed.

The first thing that ran through my mind was a story that Mommy told me. She said when she was in high school she had heard about a woman who had gone to the bathroom and a snake came out of her body. She said it came from voodoo.

The second thing that came to my mind was that I had seen enough monster movies to know that anything was possible. I stood with my back against the door of the stall. I was still screaming while I changed my pad. Cherry was in the next stall. She tried to get my attention by pounding on its dividing partition.

"What's wrong? Are you alright? Mona, what's wrong?"

"A big red blob just came out of me! It's in the toilet!"

I looked at it in horror and I was afraid of it! I counted to three and pulled the plumbing handle. It wouldn't flush! The toilet gurgled and burped. I flushed it again. Instead of the water going down, it came up. It looked as if it was going to flow over the brim. Cherry was also saying something, but I couldn't believe my ears. Perhaps I did not hear her right.

"What did you say?"

"You probably had a miscarriage!"

Just as I was about abandon my stall, everything went down. I flushed it again for good luck.

Cherry waited for me by the sink. My hands were shaking so bad that I could hardly work the handles of the faucet or operate the soap dispenser. She asked me if I was alright again. I could barely talk. I was still in shock. She stood next to me while I washed my hands. Indirectly she looked at me in the mirror and said, "Don't worry, it's no big deal. I've had two miscarriages already."

To be honest, I didn't know whether to believe her or not and she certainly did not look surprised. She was always sneaking boys in the house when her father was at work. Whatever that thing was that I flushed in the toilet couldn't have been what happened to her. I wanted to tell her that it was impossible for me to have a miscarriage because I wasn't having any relations, but what difference would it have made? She was already talking about herself and her own experiences.

It was almost time for the movie to begin. We bought candy and popcorn. At some time during the movie images in my mind began to flash before my eyes.

Perhaps it was the darkness in the movie and the stars that were up on the movie screen. For some reason, in my mind I saw another dark sky filled with stars. I also saw particles of sand along the ground. It felt as if sand was on my clothes.

As I brushed my hand from the top of my blouse to the bottom of my skirt, I could have sworn that I heard a voice say,

"How does it feel?"

The voice sounded familiar and disturbing. In the next set of images I saw myself falling into a pile of sand and then I saw a man's face. I couldn't exactly figure out who it was, and now it was flashing in and out of the strobe light of my mind.

All of a sudden it hit me like a lightning bolt. His face! I had forgotten all about him! Could Cherry have been right? All I could do was bury my face in my hands. I also tried to delete the images from my own mind, but they wouldn't go away. Cherry must have become concerned because she took hold of my arm and asked how I was. With my hands still at my face, I responded by only turning my head from side to side. When she ask me what was wrong, I nodded my head up and down and held my palms out to the movie screen and assured her that I was okay.

But I wasn't okay! Frame by awful frame a kaleidoscope of painful memories turned in different shapes and forms of that blinding nightmare. It was him! I completely forgot about him! Maybe Cherry was right. Perhaps I did have a miscarriage. I had forgotten about that night. At that point I was wishing for P.J.

I don't know how I made it through the rest of the movie. I had to force myself to concentrate because I wanted a decent grade.

On our way home I let Cherry do most of the talking. She talked on and on about some of her experiences when she was in the hospital suffering with depression. I didn't feel too well. My abdomen was still cramping. My mind was so flooded with flashbacks that I could hardly concentrate on Cherry's stories.

Cherry never did ask for his name. Nor did we talk about what I experienced in that stall. P.J. and I never spoke about that night again. Sadly, no matter how hard we try to forget some things, they have a way of coming back to us. Most likely his name sounded good on the day he was born, but now his name doesn't deserved to be remembered.

Over the years, I have tried to forget about the monkey chant. I try not to make it a habit of thinking about it. After all, we were just children, monkey see, monkey do. As poignant as it was for me, I decided to let it go. It wasn't until my eleventh-grade Spanish class that I learned that in Spanish, "Mona" means "monkey."

The finale of *Romeo and Juliet* ended in death as did the seed of my blind date. During that theatrical mishap of mine, God was still good. He performed a miracle—even when I didn't know I needed one.

CHAPTER 22

FEARFULTITIOUS

Receiving my high school diploma was not exactly a miraculous moment, but it was one of my happiest, long-awaited achievements throughout my public school years.

For all who graduated, our parting was just sweet sorrow. Although a lot of us vowed to keep in touch, I believe most of us knew in our hearts that after that day chances were we'd never see each other again.

After spending a total of fourteen years in public school, it felt as if I was the senior citizen of my class. At the time I had no real ambitions. I didn't even know what I wanted to be. All that mattered to me was that I graduated from high school. Spending the rest of my life celebrating it sounded good to me.

My parents wanted me to go to college. I believe they wanted to give me a chance at making a better future for myself. I didn't believe that I had what it took to make it in college. I know I wasn't a dumb bunny, but at that time that was how I felt.

Terry Cooper dropped out of high school and married her boyfriend because he got her pregnant. Gracie Williams graduated from high school and also got married. Little by little, our little clique broke up, but we continued to stay in touch with each other. Arlene and Angela Thomas went to college. Arlene became a teacher and Angela became a postal worker. Rex Briggs joined the navy and Roger Ward became a hippie and moved to California. A week after Emily graduated from high school she dated one of the local taxi cab drivers for one week and married him the next. Cherry ran away from home and also got married. Her husband was very handsome, but he also was abusive. The cigarette burns in her flesh were not as bad as what happened to Sandra Mitchell. I had hoped one day to meet up with her, but sadly I never got to see her green eyes again. She married a very jealous man who killed her with a hammer by pounding it on her head. I suppose she was already dead by the eighth blow. Winky prefers to be called Joel and went on to carpentry school. P.J. still is the rainbow to my heart and the only one from our clique that graduated from college.

I decided to go to a nearby county college and did two semesters. I took a business course. As the math got harder, it drew the dumb-bunny ears right out of my head just like a television antenna, except I was not receiving anything. College homework was overwhelming. If I was going to learn anything I needed a new set of rabbit ears. For the next four years I worked in factories, partied at night clubs, and continued to go to church on Sundays.

Mommy continued her membership at Trinity Baptist. Daddy graduated from seminary school. He became a local Elder and ministered at New Zion. Looking at my father's position, serving as a minister, husband, and father, I felt that I needed to give honor where it was due. I left Trinity Baptist and joined New Zion Methodist Church. I felt torn because I loved both churches.

As years went by, New Zion's membership spiraled down. By the time I joined, the majority of its members had left. The remaining members were mostly family. The church was built in 1891. It stayed pretty much nostalgic. It had a piano but no pianist. The songs we sang were straight out of the hymn book.

I taught Sunday school, served on the missionary board, and cleaned the church. I made it a habit to clean the church during the day because night was not the time to be in that church, especially by myself. At night I always felt an uncomfortable presence, as if I was in the shadows of someone else's territory. Whatever it was sometimes felt as if it was right at my face but I just could not see it. It made me feel scared and uneasy.

Daddy also felt the same presence at night when he was in that church. One night he was alone studying his sermon in the parsonage and he said that he watched two china cups leave the cupboard, move through the air, and land on the table. He said it annoyed him more than it scared him.

As a Christian, why was I experiencing fright night in a church? Whatever spirit took territory in that church, I felt it didn't want me there. Its presence was so thick that I wasn't going to challenge it, so I did all my cleaning chores for the church during the day.

For God hath not given us the spirit of fear; but of power and love and sound mind. 2nd Timothy 1:7 of the King James Bible

One meaning in the dictionary for fear is "an unpleasant often strong emotion caused by expectation or unawareness of danger." The other meaning is "a profound reverence, especially for God."

I often heard speakers say the acronym for fear is False Evidence Appearing Real.

I would be wrong if I didn't take some responsibility in feeling fearful toward certain matters. Shortly after graduating from high school, Terry Cooper and I took a train to New York City to see a movie. The weather conditions were bad. It was cold. The snow must have been a foot high. We waited in line for about an hour to see the movie. We huddled close to each other to keep warm.

We had no idea what the movie was about. We had only heard that it was a "must see." After paying for our tickets, vomit bags were issued. The ushers insisted that each viewer must take one.

What we saw in that movie was more chilling than the snow. We knew it was only a movie, but seeing that girl's head turn 360 degrees kind of freaked us out. We screamed, we jumped, we huddled tightly for comfort.

Those horrifying images in that movie were shocking. Going to the movies with a friend was a wonderful idea, but to watch that kind of movie was not.

Terry and her husband separated because she found out that he was seeing other women. She celebrated her freedom by going out to night clubs even during the week. Terry seemed troubled about the separation and even more troubled after seeing that movie in New York. That movie had such an effect on Terry that she sought refuge and went from night club hopping to church hopping. Terry was always a Baptist, but since that night at the movies, she went Pentecostal. She was in church at least three to four nights of the week.

Terry insisted that I go to church with her. At first I had reservations about going to church with her because she loved to socialize but she never cared for church. She didn't have to wear my resistance down, because after seeing that movie, my fears had also risen to a higher level.

The first time I went with her I drove my car, and the second time we went church hopping she drove her car. Terry was always talkative, but that evening she seemed preoccupied. I couldn't wait to get to the church to get away from the loud silence. The seats were already filling up, the people were already singing, and some were already clapping to the beat of the tambourines.

Terry put her pocketbook down on the seat and walked away. I thought she was going to the bathroom, but she went to the altar. At first I thought to myself, "What the...!" This was not her usual MO. Terry didn't do altars. With her eyes fixed upon the congregation she paced from one end of the altar to the other end of the altar like a lion in a cage. I knew something was wrong because she looked out of place, like a plastic cup on a shelf full of glasses. There were two women standing at the altar but now they looked worried and backed away from Terry.

She didn't even squint! Her eyes were wider than an owl's and fixed upon the congregation like a predator. When her light brown eyes fell upon me, instantly, I looked away. My ears heard a raspy, unidentifiable voice, "Who can I get into?" Honestly, I thought I was hearing things and when I looked to the altar, I could hardly believe my eyes or believe my ears! Again, "Who can I get into?" and she went from speaking in English to speaking in strange tongues and then she said it again for the third time. I was too flipped! Was I seeing and hearing things? Seeing it in the movies was one thing, but seeing it in real life was another. I wanted to get out of my seat and run out of that church.

Thank God for small favors. The pastor and deacons ran everyone out of the church as if there was a fire. They ordered the congregation to take their belongings. I saw people grabbing their Bibles, women carrying their purses, and everyone picking up their keys. Although I was with her, no one had to tell me twice. To have seen someone acting demon-possessed in the movies was scary, and to actually witness it in real life was even worse!

I went across the street and sat in Terry's car. I locked the car doors and kept the windows rolled up. The radio kept me company. I tried to doze, but I couldn't sleep. I waited for nearly four hours. Finally right when I was getting ready to doze, I heard a tap on the window of the car. It was Terry. Although it was her car, I was not going to let her in if she was still in the same condition that I last saw her. After taking a good look at her, I asked, "Are you alright, Terry?"

"Yeah, I'm alright."

"Are you sure?"

"Yeah, let me in."

I wanted to say to her "not by the hair of my chinny- chin-chin!" Since her eyes and her voice sounded normal, I took my chances and opened the car door.

After I let her in the car, I asked her again, "Terry, are you sure you are alright?"

"Yeah, I'm alright. Why?"

I could not believe she asked that question. She was the one that became demon-possessed! Just about everyone got thrown out of that church. For four hours I sat in her car while she got the demons cast out of her and now she wanted to know why I was asking if she was alright.

Instead of getting into theory I tried to keep my head straight and watched her from the corner of my eye. She turned the ignition key on and drove. The only thing I wanted was to get home safely. She seemed okay. It was as if she had come out of a coma with no recollection as to what had transpired. All the way home I remember praying to God to not let that demon return. To this day we have never spoken about that night.

When I got home I prayed my prayers and went to bed. My Bible was kept close to my heart. The look in Terry's eyes and what she had said at that altar played in my mind frame by awful frame until the crack of dawn. Like a vampire, it wasn't until then that I was able to sleep.

On the following evening I explained to my parents what had happened to Terry the previous night. Mommy's comments were, "Every church is not church. You shouldn't let just anyone put their hand on you. They could be passing demons on to you." Daddy also agreed.

About a week later, I drove my car one night and thought I saw someone in my rearview mirror. It looked like they were in the back seat of my car. Naturally I screamed. It was amazing that I did not have a heart attack. Each time I turned around to see who or what it was, I saw nothing. With my heart inside my throat, I made another attempt to look back. In doing so, my car went off the road. Finally I got a good look at the perpetrator. Lucky me! It was my beach ball.

Shortly after that I had another fright night.

It was a Bible study night held in the home of Terry's Pentecostal friends. There may have been about ten of us in that meeting. Before Bible study we stood in a circle and prayed.

In the circle, "Hallelujah!" came out of this one's mouth. "Thank you, Jesus!" came out of that one's mouth, and "Glory!" from another. All of this praise sounded pretty normal to me, but nothing could have prepared me for what I heard next.

The Evangelist Mother raised her arms in the air and announced, "Satan is in this room." Instantly my heart began to race. I didn't come here to see Satan. She was a large woman and I certainly didn't want her coming at me. I told myself that if she looked at me, I was going to run out of the door. I knew where I was and if I had to walk five miles to get home, then so be it.

The Evangelist Mother now summoned Satan to come forth. It seemed as if everyone was on the same page except me. It took a little more than five minutes, but they found their suspect.

Poor guy! His body was stretched across the floor. He coughed, spat, and growled. He looked as if he was having an epileptic seizure.

The Evangelist Mother rebuked his demons. Everyone else joined her except me. If I didn't know any better, that poor man was getting a good old-fashioned beat-down from a bunch of frustrated women. Not only did I feel sorry for him, but I was glad that I was not him.

After that day I realized that I was not ready to face my fears. Each time I ventured a spiritual quest, the devil showed up. Ever since childhood I had had that problem. After I said my prayers, the *Bogey-Man* and the *Sand-Man* were always just a light switch away from getting me or putting sand in my eyes. The same scenario still happened after I stopped believing in "those guys." I'd say my bedtime prayers, get a little snooze, and then the *Witch* would ride me.

Whether or not it was in my head or in my heels, something finally clicked. Why venture? The church where I needed to stay was practically in my own back yard.

SILENT NIGHTS, SCARY NIGHTS

Here I was, twenty-two years old and still single. It seemed as if all my friends were married except me. Again, I felt I was being left out. I wanted a husband too.

I can't say that I was totally sure about what kind of man I wanted to marry, but I was certainly sure about what kind I didn't want to marry. As matter of fact, Clayton helped me to consider some of my decisions.

He suggested that I marry someone brave. I guess it would have been silly to marry someone who also screamed at the sight of a mouse. I needed someone who was not afraid of the dark. Clayton also pointed out that I should find someone who was not afraid of responsibilities such as working and paying bills.

A few attributes of my father also influenced what I wanted to see in the man I would marry. First of all, he needed Christ as his own personal savior. I wanted someone who wasn't afraid to get his hands dirty and would at least try to repair simple things that needed repair. The man I married needed to fit that shoe. I thought about looking for the man on a white horse, but what chances would I have with him? The man on the black horse was too risky. Marrying the man on the donkey—how bad could that be? Didn't King Jesus ride on a donkey?

I met a man named Randy. He stood about eight inches taller than me and his face felt as smooth as butter. The fairness of his skin didn't matter to me, but I did hear someone say one time, "You two look like chocolate and caramel." His car had a 135–cubic-inch engine that ran only ninety horsepower. The body and the paint on the car made heads turn and made people look twice, but it was only an imitation of a hot rod.

Randy looked good, the car looked good, and they both had lots of potential. Randy played bass guitar in a local band. He brought me lots of sunshine and always promised me the moon. Regardless of what he had or didn't have, he was always the star in my show.

Shortly after P.J. graduated from college she came back home and got married. I was in her wedding and she was in mine.

Being married to Randy made me one of the happiest people in the world. To keep from arguing I'd give him "the silent treatment," which often led more to a silent night rather than a peaceful night.

Obviously I needed to learn about communication skills. After reading a few self-help books, I finally learned to use a few techniques such as respecting his opinion and meeting him halfway. I had to remind myself that I was his wife, not his psychic, and of course he wasn't a mind reader. I still practice to say what I mean without being mean when I am expressing my thoughts. I try to omit certain words from my vocabulary such as "you always" and "you never." Don't get me wrong, just because I did not use those words of absolute did not mean that I was not thinking them.

I may have found ways to communicate properly, but I didn't have my peace. Many of my dreams were only nightmares. Perhaps it came from the books I was reading or the horror movies I was watching. That type of entertainment almost destroyed me. I became very afraid of the dark. The *Witch* often visited me with a vengeance, making me feel as if it was trying to suffocate me while I was asleep. I began to always feel an unseen evil presence and I was also afraid to be alone.

I tried to conquer my fears by reading the Bible and buying spiritual self-help books. Although I put away the horror books and movies, those ghostly images were still formed in my mind.

Around that time I went on a ten-day juice fast to lose some weight. On the seventh day of my fast, after reading my Bible at the dining room table, I heard an audible voice say,

"You call yourself worshiping Me when every time the devil says 'BOO!' you jump."

I know it is hard to believe, but I was not afraid. Knowing that God is a jealous God, I felt I was being unfaithful to Him. I was giving all my fears to the enemy. Jumping at every noise I heard, who was I really worshiping? I wanted desperately to stop, but I didn't know how.

I needed someone to talk to about this new revelation but who? If I had gone to my parents, they would have probably thought I was being silly. My husband may have felt that I was crazy. I loved P.J. too much to scare and worry her. The only person I felt I could talk to was my cousin Virginia.

Virginia was also a member of New Zion. She was always a kind-spirited person. She wasn't judgmental and always gave me good advice.

One Sunday morning after church services, I told her about the voice I heard at the dining table. I also shared with her that I felt I was being watched by spirits. I told her it felt as if I was losing my mind.

"Have you ever thought what you were feeling might be your angels?"

Honestly, this was all new to me. As she continued to talk I shook my head from side to side.

"Everyone has angels. You are surrounded by them all the time. If you feel you are being watched by something, then thank God for surrounding you with His angels."

"Why don't my angels send the bad spirits away?"

"Only you can do that, but your angels are still there to protect you."

"What do you mean only I can send the bad spirits away?"

"Your fears are like magnets, drawing in all the things that you fear. If you keep your mind focused more on God, then your fears will become less."

I knew she would be the right person to go to. What she said made sense, but sometimes old habits die hard. I felt spiritually split. On one side of the coin I had faith and on the other side of the coin I had fear. I was tired of being afraid and asked God to give me a better understanding of His word. How long could I go on leaning on my own fearful understanding?

CHAPTER 23

VISIONARY

As I said before, P.J. and I have always lived somewhat parallel lives. She was hired at a pharmaceutical company and climbed the corporate ladder. I on the other hand was hired at a warehouse and climbed an industrial ladder. We were pregnant about the same time. We both wanted girls, but within five years, she birthed three boys and I birthed three boys. Shortly after birthing my second child, my mother became terminally ill and P.J.'s father also became terminally ill. They both died about a year apart.

It was a tough time for the both of us. I was four months pregnant when my mother died. Daddy did his best to prepare us for her death. There was lots of support from many family members, and by the grace of God we all got through it. As a child I don't think I could have handled it because that was one of my biggest fears. At least my mother lived long enough to see me get married and have children. I finally found peace in knowing that she was at peace and no longer in pain; those were the thoughts that helped me to ease my pain.

P.J. continued to worship at Trinity and I continued to worship at New Zion. Our hands were full. We took care of our families, we went to church, and we stayed employed.

Seeing each other was sometimes impossible. Although we phoned each other regularly, we still missed being in the company of each other. Of course, where there is a will, there is a way.

It was around 1983 when a new non-denominational church in our area began to rise. It was built outside of our home town. Their pastor was Caucasian, but he reeled in thousands of people from all kinds of denominations and whose colors were from various shades of the rainbow. P.J. said that Pastor Gillyard was a dynamic speaker on Thursday night Bible study because she had already checked him out.

On the following Thursday I rode with her to check out the hype. On that evening Pastor Gillyard really threw out the bait. I couldn't wait to share what I had seen and heard. At first he talked about casting our cares to the Lord and then he became incredibly theatrical about it. Alongside his foot was a suitcase. He took it to the altar and knelt. He explained that all his cares were in that suitcase and he had no intentions of carrying them back with him. The real eye-opener was when he picked up the suitcase anyway and carried it to show the congregation how we looked when we laid our cares on the altar and then took those same cares back with us. The pastor taught us that our circumstances were not bigger than God. He mentioned that as long as we acted like victims we would always be defeated. He talked about how our lack of faith could block our blessings.

For the next few months on Thursday nights I treated myself to joining P.J. and learning more life-changing lessons. As much as my spiritual knowledge increased, my restful nights decreased. I needed a serious breakthrough. The *Witch* rode me frequently through the night and even during the day if I was napping. The attacks were strong. I felt as if an evil spirit was holding me down. Sometimes it became difficult to breathe. It felt as if I was being suffocated. Each time the spell fell on me, I asked myself, "Why is this happening to me?" It felt like a punishment. If it was some sort of punishment, then it was certainly fruitless because I didn't know why I was being punished. Strangely, it seemed the more I studied my Bible, the harder the *Witch* would ride.

The *Witch* was not the only problem that disturbed me during my sleep. Long before my mother died, visions of expiring family members appeared. Three days before my mother died I heard in a vision the sound of a locomotive steam engine as it approached the back yard of my parents' home. The engine brakes screeched, the whistle blew once, and out came three puffs of steam. Pulling in parallel and standing as high as their house was an old black locomotive steam engine with a ghastly cow-catching grill to its front. I knew in my spirit what that dream meant. My mother's health was already taking a turn for the worse. The train meant departure and the three puffs of steam meant she had three days left.

Truly, I did not like that dream or the others that followed. A debut of world disasters appeared regularly in my dreams. I saw explosions, aircrafts crashing, earthquakes rumbling, and mudslides. The dream that disturbed me the most was a rocket ship launching straight up into the blue and then all of sudden exploding. What my eyes saw and my heart felt was the terrible loss of the rocket's crew whose lives were sacrificed in an unexpected course to their final destination. Unfortunately, on January 28, 1984, the dream materialized. The Challenger exploded and claimed the lives of six people. During that time and shortly before I saw several aircrafts crash. On September 1, 1983, another dream materialized. The South Korean Boeing 747 was shot down after violating Soviet airspace. The lives of 269 were claimed. Another vision materialized on November 27, 1983. The Colombian Boeing 747 crashed near Madrid claiming the lives of 183 people.

I have heard people say that having these visions is a gift, and I have also heard others say it is a curse. Whichever it was, it was always disturbing. Upon sharing these visions I noted for myself that I was nothing more than the messenger for bad news. For the next few years these visions continued to appear while I slept. I asked myself many times, "Why me? What is the purpose of knowing all these bad things and not being able to do anything to prevent them?"

Well...not all my visions ended in disasters. In 1988 my husband and felt it was time to look for a house. After looking at a few homes I knew exactly which one I wanted. I had already seen it in one of my dreams.

Our closing was set for Friday the thirteenth. We could have moved in on that day but our children insisted that we wait one more day. We never taught them to believe in superstitions. We never told them about the *Bogey-Man*, the *Sand-Man,* or Santa Claus. I guess their concerns were understandable being that our back yard property line was connected to the back yard of an old cemetery.

Six years after we moved into our home, my husband and I also felt it was time to look for a new place to worship. It was not an easy decision. I asked my father to give me his blessing and he did. For about two years my family joined membership with Trinity and then joined with another Methodist church.

The summer of 1994 I was invited to come to Vacation Bible School at a nearby church. The pastor was the teacher of the adult class. He asked us to do three things that week: find a project, work on it at home, and bring it in on the last day of Bible School.

Over the years I'd collected many birthday cards and post cards. For my project I decided to make a scrap book of my favorite cards. While going through my collection I came across a birthday card that my mother had given to my oldest child.

On the front of the card was a young African American boy. He sat happily on the horse of a merry-go-round. His face looked out in the direction of the crowd. His arm was stretched to feel the wind. The little boy had a head full of hair. Seeing this card was a miracle. It brought just as much joy on that day as it did when it was presented. The boy on the card was the spitting image of my child whom she had never seen. Of course I couldn't help but scream, "She did see my baby!"

TRUTH

When I was in high school I vowed to myself that when I graduated, I would work the night shift when I got hired to work. While raising my children I stayed true to that vow. To be honest, I had very little choice. I tried working afternoons, but it left me little time to be with my children. Their homework suffered and the babysitters were too costly.

My husband shunned the idea of his wife working nights. Most of the time, he described me as being cranky. I don't feel that I was that bad; however, we do not always see ourselves as other people see us.

Working the night shift may have saved me money on one hand but it cost me a lot of sleep on the other. Sleeping during the day was not always easy. The phone was forever ringing, the activities of the lawn mowers, leaf blowers, and chainsaws also kept me awake. Dogs barked from one end of the neighborhood to the other.

My cousin P.J. was very passionate about looking at soap operas. I slept only till one o'clock in the afternoon so that I could also watch them. Almost every day we phoned each other to talk about each program. Watching television till four in the afternoon was certainly entertaining; however, it shortened much of my rest.

When the children came home from school it was time to get into third gear. I helped them with their homework, prepared dinner, and did some household chores. By nine o'clock in the evening, I was back in the bed trying to get a little sleep before it was time to go to work.

For years I worked in a hospital as a nurse assistant. At work, I was like a zombie. During my break I'd find a quiet place to get some sleep. The *Witch* visited me regularly even on my break and wore its welcome out. On some nights it felt as if my supervisor or other coworkers were standing there looking at me. To have that feeling and not be able to wake up was a nightmare. Those occurrences came less when I used an alarm clock to keep me from oversleeping.

Working nights allowed me to go to church regularly. One Sunday morning I heard a profound message. It went something like this: "I don't have a problem if you tithe ten percent of your gross or ten percent of your net, but which do you prefer for God to bless you? I don't know about you, but I'd rather God bless me with a bucket full of what I gross than a bucket full of what I net. Do you give only your leftovers? I don't know about you, but I want more than God's leftovers."

My first thought was that ten percent was too much. My bills were already being paid by the skin of my teeth. As my flesh fought against tithing, a small voice within me asked, "Do you trust me?" I felt split. One half of me felt convicted and the other side rationalized why I should not tithe more.

I always knew that the biggest bubble gum machine was in the sky. I wanted to be abundantly blessed, but how could I afford to sacrifice? I compromised by settling for God's leftovers. How bad could that be? After all, how could I miss what I never had?

Although I didn't starve, I also didn't burp. I still needed a miracle in order to live more comfortably. There were times that I was tempted to not tithe, but a small voice in my head kept saying, "Do you trust me?"

I had read enough of the Bible to know that to fight against God is a losing battle. Although I trusted Him, I still wondered how I was going to pay my bills.

I believe His answer was, "One dollar at a time."

At first it didn't make sense. I needed more bread than that to pay my bills. Then it occurred to me that I should pay off the small bills first. I will be the first to admit that when I talk, I sometimes play on words; but what I didn't realize was that God also has a sense of humor. Bread was what I needed to pay my bills and bread was what I received.

My mother's uncle worked for a large bakery. He often dropped by, leaving me loads of cakes and bread. Judging from the amount given, there must have been another significant meaning to all that bread.

One of my coworkers suggested that I sell the bread for cash. If I was being tempted, I didn't want to fail the test. I wanted to be generous like my uncle. I did not have the heart to sell the bread. I freely gave what I could not use because I didn't want my blessings to turn into stone. After Jesus had fasted forty days and forty nights the Tempter came to Him and said, *"If thou be the Son of God, command that these stones be made bread."*

But He answered and said, *"It is written Man shall not live by bread alone but by every word that proceedeth out of the mouth of God."* Matthew 4:2-4

The *Witch* still attacked me while I was asleep. The attacks had gotten worse. Almost every night I was tormented. The attacks became severe and dangerous. During most of the spells it felt as if the devil was trying to suffocate me with his hands on my face. Sometimes it felt as if I was going to die.

It wasn't until the spring of 1999 that I had finally had enough! After waking up from one of those attacks, I sat up in my bed and raised my arms to God. I was angry! I felt as though I was going to lose my mind or lose my life if these attacks continued. Even though I couldn't see God, I knew that He was right there. All I could do was cry to Him.

"Where are you, God? The devil keeps putting his hand in my face. Where are my angels? Why are they watching me being tormented? Do my angels sleep when I sleep? What am I doing wrong? Do I need to give more tithes? What do You want from me?"

After screaming out those questions, I cried till I couldn't cry anymore.

When my children were young and were picked on by bullies, my advice to them was that the only way to stop the bullies was to tell on them. Why didn't I heed my own advice? One of my bullies was only a light switch away. I should have told on him a long time ago. After that conversation with God, not only did I feel better but the *Witch* became practically extinct. If there ever was a purgatory then I must have been in it. Since then the few attacks I did have weren't nearly as frightening as before.

To be a Christian and tormented by such things did not match. Since childhood I had watched horror movies with my brother. As a teenager I watched them with my friends. As an adult I have watched them with my husband. Horror movies had a lasting effect on my imagination. I thought that I was facing my fears, but in reality I was only feeding them.

I also loved drama. I lost lots of sleep behind those television soaps. Since the spring of 1999, they no longer appeal to me. I have no desire to watch anything that will rob me of my sleep.

"It is vain for you to rise up early, to sit up late and eat the bread of sorrows, for He gives his beloved sleep." Psalms 127:2

"When I was a child I spoke as a child I understood as a child but when I became a man I put away childish things." Corinthians 13:11

As a child I was afraid of the *Bogey-Man* and the *Sand-Man*. When I found out they were made-up creatures those silly fears were put away. Apparently someone thought I was bored. For seven years I had no real fears. When Valerie explained what babies see when born with a veil over their eyes, it watered and fertilized the seeds of fear, which instantly sprung up in me like popcorn.

"When the unclean spirit is gone out of a man, he walks through dry places seeking rest; and finding none, he says, I will return unto my house whence I came out." Luke 11:25

"For God has not given us the spirit of fear; but of power and love and sound mind." II Timothy 1:7

As a Christian, if we take God's word with a grain of salt, then how can we be the salt of the earth? Obviously I wasted most of my life being afraid of the wrong things.

"Therefore thou keep the commandments of the Lord thy God, to walk in his way and fear Him." Deuteronomy 8:6

God is a Jealous God. Like the three little pigs, I was scared all the time. If I wasn't scared of one thing, I was scared of another. What did I have to be afraid of?

The *Bogey-Man*.

The *Sand-Man*.

Santa's pepper.

The dark.

The *Witch*.

Rejection.

Confrontations.

Spirits.

The devil.

Not having enough bread to pay my bills.

At first tithing was hard for me to accept. The voice I had heard in my head now echoed in my heart. "Do you trust me?"

When my uncle gave me all of that bread, each slice, each loaf, and each crumb led me to a stronger trail of faith. His generosity was an example of God's goodness and His mercy. To this day I would rather tithe than lean on my own fearful understanding.

I still like television, but I will not let it rob me of sleep. My children are now grown, I no longer work the night shift, and I sleep more peacefully.

While writing this story a dear cousin from North Carolina visited my home. I shared with her what inspired me to write this book. Her advice was, "When we educate ourselves about the things we fear, it can set us free."

After hearing and learning about other sleep disorders, I put two and two together. Several years ago my cousin P.J. gave me a home edition of the *Jensen A–Z Medical Manual*. It was published by the pharmaceutical company she worked for. Much of the information I needed to know about the *Witch* was printed in the book. At the time I had only read what was written on sleep apnea and another sleeping condition called narcolepsy.

In December 2008 I had an appointment with my doctor. After I was physically examined, I discussed with her the terrifying paralysis that sometimes happened to me when I was asleep.

"Dr. Dubinsky, sometimes after I go to sleep, I experience the feeling of being paralyzed, and when I try to wake up, I can't move. Sometimes I cannot tell if I'm imagining things that aren't there. It's really scary."

Dr. Dubinsky answered, "It's called cataplexy."

"Ca-ta-what?"

"Cataplexy."

"Do you mean it has a name?"

"Yes, it's called cataplexy. It's a good thing that you can't move."

"Why is that a good thing? That's the scariest thing!"

"Your body is keeping you from acting out your dreams. That's why you cannot move."

It took a few seconds for that information to sink into my head. I could not believe the *Witch* had a medical name. For a long time I thought I was going crazy. For years I thought I was cursed. Then she went on to say, "The images you thought you saw or heard are called hypnogogic hallucinations. If it happens upon going to sleep it's called hypnogogic hallucinations. If it happens upon awaking it's called hypnopompic."

I had wanted answers, and there they were. It felt as if something had been lifted off of me. I thanked her graciously for giving me that information. I really wanted to hug her, but I held on to my composure because the word "cataplexy" sounded too much like catatonia and I didn't want the doctor to take me away in a straightjacket.

Before the doctor left the examination room I jokingly asked, "You mean this thing wasn't caused by a witch?

She just looked at me and smiled. I guess I was lucky that she didn't call security to have me taken away.

I celebrated this new revelation as I drove home. I was as happy as the three little pigs when they sang "Who's afraid of the big bad wolf?" At that time I was also writing this book. I had no idea how I was going to end it without some kind of medical name for my sleep disorder. I couldn't wait to get home so I could share this knowledge with my husband and children. They were just as surprised as I was to hear that my sleep disorder was always a medical condition.

I suppose I could spend the rest of my life blaming others for my fears and shortcomings, but what good would that do?

There were many lessons that needed to be remembered, habits that needed to be broken, and fears I needed to face.

My mother called the sleeping disorder the *Witch*. Its medical terminology is cataplexy.

I am not a medical expert, nor am I a theologian, but based on scriptures I would say that cataplexy comes from "the spirit of fear."

To avoid cataplexy I stay away from horror movies especially before I go to sleep. If I take a nap and need to wake up in an hour or two then I set the clock. I make a habit of getting the proper sleep and rest I need.

I am not as jumpy as I used to be. Sometimes fear will still try to make its call, but in most cases I let it fall on deaf ears. The voice of fear is often loud while the voice of Jesus is still a small voice. In the first few verses of the Bible in Saint John chapter ten, Jesus explains that if we are His sheep then we will hear His voice.

Almost all my life I hoped to receive miracles rolling from that big bubble gum machine in the sky. Little did I know that I too could be a bubble gum machine. Now that I am emptied of all those old fears, I can let God be the vendor of my soul.

He embraces me with His love and restores my soul. He fills me with His spirit and gives me all kinds of wisdom. Knowing that His mercy endures forever, I can live my life in faith and not in fear. I have peace even when I am in a storm.

As a church nurse I often assist in giving first aid and comfort to whoever needs it. Children often look at me as if I am going to take their tonsils or poke them with a hypodermic needle. Wearing my white uniform, white nylons, and white shoes often looks scary to them. I try my best to always smile genuinely because they know a plastic smile when they see one.

I have also had the privilege of working in mental health. I have seen the *Bogey-Man* in many of the patients I cared for.

Thanks to my father's principle, I have learned that a little smile goes a long way. Many times I am asked, "Aren't you scared to work with the mentally ill?"

I tell them the truth: "I have been around it all my life."

Danger is always present when caring for the mentally ill. However, the good outweighs the bad.

As a child I loved my Little Red Riding Hood costume. I always felt protected when I wore it. Although my little red costume is long gone, I know that it's the spirit of God that really protects me.

Recently one of the patients asked, "Mona, why aren't you smiling?"

I answered him and said, "Who do you think I am? Mona Lisa?"

Not only did he answer; everyone in ear range answered, "YES! You are Mona Lisa."

THE MULBERRY BUSH

I am grateful for the many people God has placed in my life. From each person something has always been learned, even if it was to stay away from them. Those kinds of individuals are sometimes like sandpaper when they rub me the wrong way, but I know I am not perfect and sometimes their roughness has a way of also smoothing me out.

As a child it was Clayton that comforted me. Now I have the peace of God. I believe I am much braver than I used to be. Am I still afraid of mice? I am not going to answer that question because God is not through with me yet.

Many of my friends are now divorced, remarried, or widowed. Winky has always been a good brother. Maybe someday he will get married, but in the meantime, he is like a wonderful Santa

Claus to my family. His gifts are always thoughtful and put a smile on everyone's face. I am contented in my marriage and I don't feel I've been left behind.

Once a year a group of us Mulberry patrons gather together and have a good old-fashioned barbeque and back yard party. Everyone that comes brings food. We laugh, dance, and sing, and swim. As we reminisce, it's always good to hear, "Remember when…"

Coming together as one makes our hearts rejoice as it did when we were children. I know it sounds silly, but when we are all together it feels as if we are going around the mulberry bush. Being with loving friends is more than just a blast from the past; it's also a glimpse of heaven.

Sometimes I still visit La-La Land. Don't worry! I make those trips short and sweet. I am not willing to pay the price for staying there. When I go to bed I still say my prayers. I can't wait till the lights are out. "If I die before I wake" doesn't scare me anymore, nor "Though I walk through the valley of the shadow of death, I fear no evil." The *Witch* doesn't scare me the way it used to. When I am attacked by sleep paralysis I can bring myself out of it easier than I could in the past. God is always with me when the lights are out. Some of my best ideas come when my head is on my pillow.

Before I lay me down to sleep, there is one thing I'd like for you to remember. My first name is Mona and Lisa is not my middle name. However, if you call me "Mona Lisa" I hope it makes you smile, so that I can do the same.

All right, now that we are all smiling, let me say my prayers.

Now I lay me down to sleep
I pray the Lord my soul to keep
If I die before I wake,
I pray the Lord my soul to take

SWEET DREAMS!

ROAD TO RECOVERY

A note from the author:

My first battle with sleep paralysis began when I was eight years old. It felt as if someone was holding me down. My mother said it was the *Witch* that holds you down while you are sleeping. Others may know it as the "hag." For many years I blamed my sleep paralysis on the *Witch* and then the devil. I felt powerless to stop this malevolent spirit creature. My freedom from the *Witch* began when I gained full knowledge of the truth about my sleep disorder. I believe I will always have to stay mindful of the situations that can trigger unwelcomed symptoms of sleep paralysis. My hope is that my book will bring an understanding about how some of our fears begin. By not remembering, we often repeat the mistakes of our parents and pass some of our silly fears to our own children. Every child deserves a good night's sleep and not a fearful one.

FREQUENTLY ASKED QUESTIONS

Q) What is sleep paralysis?
A) Sleep paralysis is a sleeping disorder that either occurs just when falling asleep or immediately upon waking. The person experiences a sense of wanting to move but is unable to do so. The experience can be terrifying.

Q) Can sleep paralysis be fatal?
A) Sleep paralysis is not fatal, but does the phrase "scared to death" mean anything? Fear can raise the level of your heart rate. Although sleep paralysis is not harmful, who is to say what fear can do?

Q) Can sleep paralysis be harmful?
A) The experience of someone sitting on your chest or feeling as if you are being suffocated is frightening. For centuries it was believed that this paralyzing experience was caused by the "hag/witch" phenomena. Although tales and folklore of these experiences have caused people much anxiety and fear, there is no physical harm.

Q) What can be done to alleviate sleep paralysis?
A) Talk to your doctor about your condition. This condition is treatable and curable.

Q) What brings on sleep paralysis?
A) Stress, changes in lifestyle, and sleep deprivation.

Q) How can sleep paralysis be prevented?
A) In my personal experience I have avoided sleep paralysis by:
- Getting enough sleep each night
- Avoiding sleeping on my back
- Maintaining a regular sleeping schedule
- Using an alarm clock has helped alleviate the fear of oversleeping especially when napping
- Reducing stress by choosing my battles wisely
- Eating healthier
- Avoiding horror movies and not listening to or reading that kind of material No television on while sleeping
- Talking about my fears to someone

Q) Why isn't sleep paralysis commonly talked about?
A) Although this frightening sleep disorder is regularly experienced by more than a third of the world population, it is mostly believed to be a form of curse.

Q) Why do people of folklore refer to sleep paralysis as the *Witch*?
A) Often people fear what they do not understand. During the Salem witch trials, people did not share their paralyzing experiences for fear of getting burned at the stakes.

Q) Why do people of folklore refer to sleep paralysis as being "the old hag"?
A) In the tales of folklore, "the old hag" is a malevolent witch. To be "hag-ridden" means to have been assaulted by a witch in spirit while sleeping. Many cultures from every race, creed, and color are affected and believe that the "hag" comes to sit on their bodies in an effort to entrap their souls.